"I'm sorry, I don't remember you," Anna told him softly.

"But in a way I do," she continued. "I can sense that there's something very special between us."

"You can sense that?" Ward queried, his voice suddenly disconcertingly gruff when he had intended it to sound sarcastic.

"Yes, I can," Anna confirmed. And then, to Ward's bemusement, she reached out and touched his face.

Anna quite plainly thought they were lovers, which was ironic when Ward thought of the real relationship between them.

What was taxing him was the apparent change in Anna's character. Did bumps on the head and amnesia do that?

Dear Reader,

Revenge is a very strong emotion. The need to seek it and the act of avenging a wrongdoing is very empowering. The four women in this, my latest, miniseries, all have to handle this most powerful of emotions, each in her own special way.

I am aware of the dangers of becoming blinded to everything but one single, obsessive goal. As I wrote these four books I discovered that my heroines, Kelly, Anna, Beth and Dee, all share my instincts. Like me, they desperately want to see justice done, but—also like me—they come to recognize that there is an even stronger drive: love can conquer all.

The four women share a bond of friendship, and it is very much in my mind when I write that you, the reader, and I, the writer, share a very special and personal bond, too. I invite you to share in the lives, hopes and loves of Kelly, Anna, Beth and Dee. Through love they will discover true happiness.

Penny Jordan

SWEET REVENGE ~~REVENGE~~ *Seduction*

They wanted to get even. Instead they got...married!

Look out next month for Beth's story
A Treacherous Seduction (#2074)

PENNY JORDAN

Lover by Deception

Seduction
SWEET ~~REVENGE~~

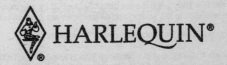

HARLEQUIN®

TORONTO • NEW YORK • LONDON
AMSTERDAM • PARIS • SYDNEY • HAMBURG
STOCKHOLM • ATHENS • TOKYO • MILAN • MADRID
PRAGUE • WARSAW • BUDAPEST • AUCKLAND

ISBN 0-373-12068-0

LOVER BY DECEPTION

First North American Publication 1999.

Copyright © 1999 by Penny Jordan.

Visit us at www.romance.net

Printed in U.S.A.

CHAPTER ONE

PAIN, anger and guilt—right now, looking at his twenty-two-year-old half-brother, Ritchie, Ward felt them all.

'Why on *earth* didn't you come to me if you needed money?' he demanded tersely.

The sunlight through the narrow, almost monastic window of Ward's study touched Ritchie's hair, turning it to bright gold.

Ward already knew that when Ritchie raised his head to look at him his blue eyes would be full of remorse.

'You've already done so much, given me so much,' Ritchie told him in the quiet, well-modulated voice that was so very much his own father's, Ward's stepfather's.

'I didn't want to bother you, to ask you for any more, but this postgraduate year in America would just be so valuable,' he told Ward earnestly, and then he was off, completely absorbed as his enthusiasm for his subject, his studies, overwhelmed his earlier guilt.

As he listened to him Ward looked at him steadily, his eyes not blue like Ritchie's and his stepfather's, but instead a dark iron-grey, the same colour as those of the tough young apprentice who had fathered him forty-two years ago and who had then lost his life before he, Ward, was out of nappies. He'd been killed in an industrial accident which had had more to do with him being the victim of a greedy employer's refusal to make sure that he was operating proper safety standards for his workforce than any genuine 'accident.' That had been in the days before such incidents were fully monitored, when any compensation for the loss of a life, a husband, a father, was at the discretion of the employer rather than a matter for the law.

Ward's mother had received nothing—less than nothing since; following her young husband's death she had had to leave the company-owned terraced property they had lived in and she and her baby son had had to move to another part of the northern town where they lived to make their home with her own parents. Baby Ward had been left with his grandmother whilst his mother earned what little she could cleaning.

It had been through her job cleaning the local school where Ward went that she had ultimately met her second husband, Ritchie's father.

She had spent a long time discussing with Ward her hopes and plans and the changes they would make to both their lives before she had accepted the proposal of the gentle English teacher who had fallen in love with her.

Neither of them had expected that their marriage would result in the birth of their own child and Ward could well understand why both of them should have been so besotted with their unexpected and precious son.

Ritchie was his father all over again. Gentle, mild-mannered, a scholar, unworldly and easily duped by others, not through any lack of intelligence but more because neither of them could conceive of the extent of other people's greed and selfishness, since these were vices they simply did not possess.

It had been thanks to his stepfather and his care, his love, his *fatherliness*, that Ward had been persuaded to stay on at school and then, later, to start out and found his own business.

He was, as others were very fond of saying, very much a self-made man. A millionaire now, able to command whatever luxuries he wished since the communications business he had built up had been bought out by a large American corporation, but Ward preferred to live simply, almost monastically.

A big lion of a man, with broad shoulders and the tough-hewn body and bone structure he had inherited from his own father and through him from generations of working men, gave him a physical appearance of commanding strength and presence. Other men feared him—and their women...

His dark eyebrows snapped together angrily, causing his silently watching half-brother to wince inwardly and wish that he had not been so foolish.

Only the other week Ward had had to make it sharply plain to the wife of a business colleague that despite her obvious sensuality and availability he was not interested in what she had to offer.

Ward had grown up with a mother who was everything that a woman should be—tender, loving, gentle, loyal and trustworthy.

It had come as an unpleasant awakening to discover how rare her type of woman actually was.

His wife, the girl he had fallen in love with and married at twenty-two, had shown him that. She had left him before their marriage was a year old, declaring that she preferred a man who knew how to have fun, a man who had time and money to spend on her.

By that time Ward had been as disillusioned by marriage as she, tired of coming home to an empty house, tired of having to search through empty cupboards to throw himself a meal together, but tired most of all of a woman who gave nothing to their relationship or to him but who took everything.

Even so, it had given him very little pleasure five years later to have her feckless husband come begging him for a job.

More out of disgust than anything else he had not just given him one but had made the couple a private, non-repayable 'loan.' He could still remember the avaricious look he had seen in his ex-wife's eyes as she'd looked around the new house he had just moved into, assessing the worth of the property, of the man who could have been hers.

Small wonder, perhaps, that she had had the gall to dare to come on to Ward behind her new husband's back, claiming that she had loved him all along and that their divorce, her desertion of him, had been an aberration, a silly mistake. Even if he'd had the misfortune to still love her, which fortunately he did not, Ward would not have taken her back. It was in his genes, his tough northern upbringing and inheritance, to prize loyalty and honesty above all else.

Their marriage was dead, he had told her starkly, and so too was whatever emotion he had once felt for her.

He hadn't seen her since, nor had he wished to do so, and since then he had opted for a woman-free lifestyle, but that of course did not mean that he didn't have his problems, and he was being confronted with one of them right now.

When Ritchie had won a place at Oxford, Ward had proudly and willingly offered to finance him. Ritchie was, after all, his half-brother, his family, and Ward himself could never forget the help and support his stepfather had given *him* when he was first getting started.

His parents, *their* parents, were retired now, his stepfather, older than their mother by nearly fifteen years, in poor health, suffering from a heart condition, which meant that he had to live as quietly as possible, without any stress. Which was why...

'Why the *hell* didn't you *tell* me you needed more money?' he reiterated to Ritchie explosively now.

'You'd already given me so much,' Ritchie repeated. 'I just couldn't—didn't...'

'But for God's sake, Ritchie, surely your intelligence, your common sense *must* have told you that the whole thing was a scam? No one, but no one, pays that kind of interest or gets that kind of return. Why the hell do you think they were using the small ads?'

'It just seemed to be the answer to my problem,' Ritchie told him. 'I had the five thousand that you'd given me in the bank, and if it could be turned into virtually ten in a matter of months and I could get a holiday job as well...' He stopped uncomfortably as he saw the way Ward was shaking his head and looking skyward in obvious angry disbelief.

'It seemed such a good idea,' he insisted defensively. 'I had no idea...'

'You're dead right you didn't,' Ward agreed grimly. '*No* idea whatsoever. You should have come to me instead... Tell me again just what happened,' he instructed his half-brother.

Ritchie took a deep breath.

'There was an ad in one of those free news sheet things. I just happened to pick it up. I forget where. It said that anyone interested in seeing real growth and profit on their capital should apply to a box number they quoted for more details.'

'A box number.' Ward raised his eyes skyward a second time. 'So you, with the common sense of a lemming, applied.'

'It seemed such a good idea,' Ritchie protested again, a hurt look in his eyes. 'And I just thought...Well, Dad's always going on about how lucky I am to have you behind me, helping me, financing me. How he and Mum couldn't have afforded to give me any help to go up to Oxford and the fact that I don't have to finance myself with part-time work means that I'm free to study properly, and sometimes that makes me feel...Well, I hate thinking that Dad's comparing me to you and finding me wanting and that my classmates reckon I'm spoiled rotten because I've got *you* to bankroll me.'

Ritchie found wanting? Ward's frown deepened. He admired and respected his stepfather, yes, and loved him too, but he had always been sensitively conscious of how far short he must fall of the kind of ideals on which his gentle, unmaterialistic stepfather had founded his life.

'Anyway,' Ritchie continued, 'eventually I had a phone call from this chap and he told me what to do— said that I should send him a cheque for five thousand pounds and that he'd send me a receipt and a monthly statement showing the value of my investment. He also said he'd send me a portfolio listing where my money had been invested.'

'And did he, by any chance, also tell you just *how* he was able to offer such a reality-defying rate of growth and profit on this investment?' Ward enquired with awful ominous calm.

'He said it was because he cut out the middle man and that due to all the changes going on in certain overseas markets there were good opportunities there for those who knew the markets to make a real killing...'

'Indeed, and he, out of sheer generosity, intended to share that knowledge with anyone who happened to respond to his ad. Was that it…?'

'I…I didn't enquire into his motivation,' Ritchie responded with desperate dignity and a betrayingly flushed face.

'Oh, I know I ought to have done, but Professor Cummins had just told me that if I took this extra year out to get an additional qualification in the US, then I'd have a much better chance of success if I ever decided I wanted to apply for a fellowship over here, and he had just asked me to do some research for him for a series of lectures he was giving in America. God knows why he chose me. My grades…'

'He chose you for very much the same reason that our enterprising entrepreneur and financial crook chose you, Ritchie,' Ward told him with cool sarcasm before prodding his half-brother.

'So, to continue, you paid over the five thousand pounds you had in your bank account, and then what?'

'Well, for the first two months everything went well. I got statements showing an excellent return on the investment, but then the third month I didn't receive a statement, and when I eventually rang the number I'd been given I was told that it was unobtainable.'

He looked so perplexed that in any other circumstances Ward, who had a good sense of humour, would have been tempted to laugh a little at his naivety, but this was no laughing matter. This was a young man who had been deliberately and cold-bloodedly relieved of five thousand pounds by as shrewd a fraudulent operator as Ward had ever come across, and he had met his fair share of the breed in his time, although needless to say none of them had ever taken *him* in.

'How surprising,' was the only comment he allowed himself to make.

Ritchie raised stricken eyes to his and muttered, 'I know. I know what you're thinking but...Well, at first I just thought it was a mistake. I wrote to the address on the statements but my letter came back ''address unknown'' and since then...'

'Since then your friendly investment manager has proved that it isn't just money he can magic away into thin air?' Ward suggested dryly.

'I really am sorry, Ward, but I...I had to tell you...I haven't even got enough money left to cover myself this term now, never mind next, and...'

'How much is it going to cost you to pay for the rest of your year's living and studying expenses?' Ward asked him point-blank.

Reluctantly Ritchie told him.

'And how much for your year in the US? And I want the full cost of it, please, Ritchie, not some ridiculous guestimate because you're too proud to tell me the full amount.'

Again, this time even more reluctantly, Ritchie gave Ward the figure he wanted.

'Right,' Ward announced, opening a drawer to his desk and removing his cheque book, which he promptly opened, writing across the top cheque an amount which not only covered the sum Ritchie had disclosed but included a very generous allowance over it as well.

So much so that when he handed Ritchie the cheque the younger man gasped and coloured up to the roots of his fair hair, protesting, 'No, Ward, I can't. That's far too much... I...'

'Take it...' Ward overrode him firmly and then glanced at his watch before adding casually, 'Oh, and by the way, I've decided it's time you had a new car. I've got the keys for you so you can leave the old one here; I'll dispose of it for you.'

'A new car? But I don't need one; the Mini is fine for my needs,' Ritchie protested.

'For yours, yes, but your father isn't getting any younger. I know how much he looks forward to your visits home and how much he worries, and we both know that that isn't good for him. He'll feel much happier if he knows you're driving something that's safe…'

Shaking his head, Ritchie accepted the set of keys his elder brother was extending to him. There was no point in arguing with Ward. No point whatsoever. As he smiled his thanks into his brother's austerely handsome face he wished, not for the first time, that he could be more like him.

Only the previous term, when Ward had come down to visit him, one of the other students in his year, a girl—the prettiest and most sought after girl on the campus—had commented breathlessly to him that Ward was just so-o-o hunkily sexy, and Ritchie had known exactly what she meant.

There was an energy, a power, and *maleness* about Ward that somehow or other set him apart from other men. He was a born leader and he possessed that magical spark inherited from his forebears which Ritchie knew he could never, ever possess, no matter how many academic qualifications he obtained.

After his half-brother had left, Ward picked up the small folder he had brought with him. In it were the statements Ritchie had referred to. Frowningly Ward studied them. He would check out the stock they cited, of course, but he knew already that they would either be completely fictitious or, if real, never actually bought. That was how this kind of scum worked.

Heavens, but you'd have thought that a young man with Ritchie's brains would have known immediately that the whole thing was a scam. There had been enough warnings over the years in the financial press about this type of thing, but then Ritchie was studying the classics and Ward doubted that he had ever read a financial article in his life.

His father was similarly naive and had been hopelessly out of place in the large, sprawling urban jungle of a school where he had taught and where Ward himself had been a pupil. Ward had perfectly understood what his mother had meant when she had told her son gently that one of the reasons she wanted to accept Alfred's proposal of marriage was that she felt he needed someone to look after him properly.

Ward could still remember how some of the other boys had mocked and taunted him because their softie of an English teacher was now his stepfather, but Ward had soon shown them the error of their ways. He had been big and strong for his age, with a tongue that could be just as quick and painful as his fists when it needed to be.

Ward had grown up in an environment where you had to be tough to survive, and the lessons he had learned there had equipped him very well when it had come to surviving in business. But now those early thrusting, exhausting years were over. Now he never needed to work again.

He got up and walked over to stare out of the window. Down below, the Yorkshire moors rolled away towards the town. The stone manor house he had made his home was considered by many to be too bleak for comfort, but Ward just shrugged his shoulders at their criticism. It suited him. But then, perhaps, he was a bleak person. He certainly was one it wasn't advisable to try to cheat.

He looked again at the statement. He suspected that J. Cox and A. Trewayne, whoever they might be, were by now very safely out of reach; that was the way of such things. But the streak of stubbornness and the drive for justice that were such a strong part of his personality refused to allow him to dismiss the matter without making at least some attempt to bring them to book.

Now that he had sold his business, his time was pretty much his own. There were certain calls upon it, of course. He made regular visits to his parents, who were now living happily and genteelly in the spa town of Tunbridge Wells. He took a very vigorous interest in the local workshop he had founded and funded which taught youngsters the basic mechanics of a wide range of trades—thus not only providing them with some skills but also providing older men who had been made redundant with a new job which gave them a renewed sense of pride in their trades.

It was a project to which Ward devoted a considerable amount of his time, and he had no time for shirkers. Everyone accepted onto it, whether as a teacher or a pupil, was expected to work and work hard. Tucked away at the back of Ward's mind was the possibility that, should the right opportunity arise, it might be worthwhile establishing an eclectic workforce comprising the best of his young trainees and encouraging them to work both as a supportive group and on their own.

'Ward, you can't finance the apprenticeship of every school-leaver in Yorkshire,' his accountant had protested when Ward had first mooted his plans to him.

But Ward had shaken his head and told him simply, 'Maybe not, but at least I'll be able to give some of them a chance.'

'And what about those who are simply using your scheme, your generosity—the ones who are using *you*?' his accountant had asked him.

Ward had merely shrugged, the movement of his big shoulders signifying that they were broad enough to take such small-mindedness and greed. But if either his accountant or anyone else had ever dared to suggest that he was an idealist, a romantic at heart who wanted only to see the best in everyone, to help everyone, Ward would have dismissed such a statement instantly with a pithily scathing response.

He frowned as he studied the papers Ritchie had given him again and then flicked through his phone book, looking for the number of the very discreet and professional service he sometimes used when he wanted to make enquiries about anyone. As a millionaire and a philanthropist he was constantly being approached for financial help, and whilst Ward was the first man to put his hand in his pocket to help a genuinely deserving cause or person he was street-wise enough to want to make sure that they *were* genuinely deserving.

Whilst he was waiting for his call to be answered, his attention was caught by some papers awaiting his attention on his desk.

They carried his full name—once the bane of his life and the cause of many a childhood scuffle; where he had grown up there had sometimes been only one way of convincing his jeering taunter that the name Hereward did not mean that he was a victim or an easy target for the school's bullies.

Hereward.

'Why?' he had once emotionally demanded of his mother.

'Because I like it,' she had told him with her loving smile. 'I thought it suited you. Made you different…'

'Aye, it's done that all right,' he had agreed bluntly.

Hereward Hunter.

Perhaps deep down inside his mother had been motivated by much the same impulse that had driven the absentee father in Johnny Cash's famous song 'A Boy Named Sue.' She had known, not that it would make him different, but that it would make him strong. Well, strong he undoubtedly was, certainly strong enough to ensure that J. Cox and A. Trewayne paid back every penny they had gulled from his naive half-brother, even if he had to up-end them and shake them by the seat of their pants to make their pockets disgorge it.

A single bar of sunlight streaming in through the narrow window of his office touched his thick dark brown hair, burnishing and highlighting the very masculine planes of his face. His eyes were as cold and dark as the North Sea on a stark winter's day when he told the girl who answered his call whom he wanted to speak with.

Oh, yes, J. Cox and A. Trewayne were most definitely going to regret cheating his half-brother. Legally it might be possible to pursue them through the courts for fraud, but Ward had already decided that they merited something a little swifter and more punitive than the slow process of the law.

Like the bullies who had tried it on with him at school, their type relied on their victim's vulnerability and fear—not, of course, fear of violence, but of being publicly branded either foolish or, even worse, finan-

cially incompetent. And that fear prevented the truth of
what these con men were doing from being disclosed.

Well, they were soon going to discover that in trying
to con *his* half-brother they had made the biggest mistake of their grubbily deceitful lives.

CHAPTER TWO

'ANNA! Hello! How are you?'

As Anna Trewayne heard the pleasure in Dee's voice her heart skipped a small, uncomfortable beat. Dee wasn't going to sound anything like so happy once Anna had broken the news to her that she had to break.

Unhappily, she wondered whether the three of them—Dee, Kelly and herself—would have taken the decision they had taken to try to bring to book the man who had so nearly destroyed the life and broken the heart of the fourth member of their closely-knit quartet—her own god-daughter, Beth—if they had known just how things were going to turn out.

Kelly, the first of them to pit herself against Julian Cox and reveal him as the cheat and liar that he was, even with Dee's encouragement and backing, had in the end not been able to go through with their plan to unmask him by pretending to be a rich heiress. Yes, Julian had shown an interest in her, and, yes, he had also made overtures to her whilst still paying court to his existing girlfriend. But then Kelly had fallen in love, and, as Dee had generously acknowledged, there had been no way she could have continued with their plan to unmask Julian once Kelly had fallen in love with Brough and he with her.

And so Dee had announced that they would take their plan to stage two, which meant that she, Anna, had had to intimate to Julian that she would like his financial advice. She had, she had told him when they had met

19

up, a sizeable sum of money she wanted to invest to produce a good return.

Coached by Dee, who had also supplied the fifty thousand pounds Anna supposedly wanted to invest, Anna had listened wide-eyed and apparently naively whilst Julian, true to form, had informed her that he knew just the deal for her and that all she had to do was to write him a cheque for fifty thousand pounds and relax.

'Fifty thousand pounds, Dee,' Anna had protested when she had reported this conversation to her. 'It seems such a lot...'

'Not really.' Dee had stopped her firmly. Although at thirty-seven Anna was Dee's senior by seven years, Dee's mature and businesslike manner often made Anna feel that she was the younger one.

As a foursome they were perhaps a disparate group, she recognised. Beth, at twenty-four, was a dreamer, gentle and easy-going, which was what had made her such an easy victim for Julian Cox.

Kelly, Beth's friend and business partner in the pretty shop they ran in the small town of Rye-on-Averton, where Anna had encouraged them to move and open up a business, was much more vivacious and impetuous. Brough and she would make a very good couple, Anna acknowledged.

Dee was their landlady; she owned the building which housed the shop and the flat above it where both girls had lived until Kelly had met Brough. Dee's father had been a very well thought of local entrepreneur and had been on several local charity committees until his unexpected death just as Dee had been about to leave university. Immediately Dee had changed her plans, and instead of pursuing her own choice of career she had come home to take up the reins of her father's business. It had been Dee who had been the prime motivator in their decision to bring Julian Cox to book for the way he had humiliated and hurt Beth, although Beth herself was still unaware of this decision.

'We won't say anything about any of this to Beth,' Dee had informed them. 'It wouldn't serve any useful purpose and it could even do some harm, especially now that she seems to be getting over Julian and putting what happened behind her.'

'Yes, she does. She's tremendously excited about this glass she's found in the Czech Republic,' Kelly had agreed, and Anna had been too relieved to hear that Beth was getting over the pain that Julian had caused her to want to protest or argue.

It had been Dee's idea to persuade Beth to visit Prague on a buying trip after the break-up of her relationship with Julian Cox.

Since her return Beth had thrown herself into the shop with a determination and single-mindedness which had rather surprised Anna, who was more used to her god-daughter's dreamy habit of allowing others to take a leading role in things.

Perhaps she felt that now that Kelly was soon to be married it was down to her to become the senior partner in their business, Anna decided. She herself was the oldest member of the quartet; Beth's mother was her own cousin, which was how she had originally come to be asked to be Beth's godmother. Both families were based in Cornwall and had been for several generations.

At twenty-two Anna had married her childhood sweetheart, Ralph Trewayne. They had been so much in love. So very happy together. Ralph had been a quiet, gentle boy, their love for one another a very youthful, tender one. What it might have grown into, how it would have weathered the tests of time, they'd never had the opportunity to find out. Ralph had been killed; drowned whilst out sailing. They had only been married a very short time and after his death Anna had been unable to bear the sight of the sea or the memories it brought her and so she had moved here to Rye to make a new life for herself. Rye was inland and the river that ran close by was shallow and placid. Even so, Anna had deliberately chosen to buy a house outside the town, and with no views from any of its windows of the river.

Dee had commented on this once in some surprise when the subject had been raised. 'Well, this house is certainly in a lovely spot, Anna, but most people who move to Rye look upon properties in a riverside location as being in a prime position.'

Anna had seen that Dee was curious about her decision but she had simply not felt she had known her well enough at that stage to confide her feelings to her.

'This house suits me,' was all she had felt able to say. 'I like living here.'

'Well, you've certainly made a very comfortable home of it,' Dee had responded approvingly.

Ralph had been very well insured, and financially Anna was comfortably off. She had never had any desire to remarry. Somehow it would have seemed a betrayal, not so much of their love, which had now faded to a soft, fuzzy, out-of-focus memory she could sometimes scarcely believe was hers, but of the fact that Ralph was no longer alive, that his life was over, cut off cruelly short. And yes, a part of her somehow felt guilty because she *was* alive and he wasn't.

She was sad not to have had children but she enjoyed living in Rye. She liked the town's quiet pace and the beauty of its surrounding countryside. She enjoyed walking and was a member of a rambling club. Needlework was one of her hobbies, and she was currently working on a communal project involving a tapestry depicting the history of the town.

For the past five years she had been doing voluntary work, helping to provide community care for the elderly, and through her friendship with Dee she had found herself being co-opted onto several charity committees.

'I'm not quite sure I shall be very much use,' she had protested when Dee had first asked her to join one of them.

That had been in the early days of what had then been more of an acquaintanceship than a friendship, and Anna, who was normally rather retiring and reticent about making new friends, had surprised herself a little at the speed with which she had become so close to Dee. Despite Dee's outward air of self-sufficiency, Anna sensed there was an inner, hidden vulnerability about the younger woman that touched her own sensitive emotions. She liked Dee and she respected her and she acknowledged that it was Dee's energy and insistence that had encouraged her to become more involved with the town and its activities.

'Nonsense,' Dee had told her sternly. 'You undervalue yourself far too much,' she had scolded Anna, and, with Dee's encouragement, Anna had even taken the step of starting to train for voluntary counselling work. What was more, she had surprised herself by discovering how instinctively skilled she was at it.

She had her cat and her dog, and her small circle of friends, and all in all she was quite satisfied with her gentle, compact way of life. Yes, it might lack excitement and passion and love, but Ralph's death had caused her so much pain and despair that she had been afraid of allowing herself to love another man.

All in all, until Julian Cox had become involved in their lives, she had considered herself to be very content. And now here she was, feeling anything but content, dreading having to give Dee the bad news. She knew there were those who considered Dee to be too businesslike, too distant, but Anna knew there was another side to Dee—a softer emotional side.

Taking a deep breath, she announced, 'Dee, I'm afraid I've got some bad news. It's about Julian Cox and…and the money…your money…'

'He hasn't backed out of advising you on investing it, has he?' Dee asked her sharply. 'Although it has taken some time to lure him in, I thought he'd well and truly taken our bait.'

'No. He hasn't backed out,' Anna told her, 'but…'

She paused and cleared her throat. There was just no easy way for her to tell Dee this.

'Dee, he's disappeared, and he's taken the money, your fifty thousand pounds, with him.'

'He's *what*?'

'I know, I'm sorry; it's my fault…' Anna began guiltily, but Dee stopped her immediately.

'Of course it isn't your fault. How could it be? I was the one… Tell me exactly what has happened, Anna.'

Anna took another deep breath.

'Well, I did as you'd said, and I told Julian that I'd got fifty thousand pounds to invest and that I wanted a good return on it. He said he knew just the right kind of investment for me. He also suggested that we keep things very informal. He said that the deal he had in mind was an off-shore thing—something to do with

Hong Kong—and he said that the less paperwork involved, the better the profit would be for both of us.

'I did try to ring you to get your advice but you...'

'I was in London on business. I know. I picked up your message, but even if I'd been here it wouldn't have made any difference because I would most certainly have told you to go ahead.'

'Well, I agreed to what Julian was suggesting and wrote him the cheque. I thought that the mere fact that it would have to go through my bank account and his would be proof that he had had the money. He said he'd be in touch. I hadn't really intended to ring him at all— after all, it was only last week that I gave him the cheque—but then I bumped into Brough's sister Eve with your cousin Harry and she just happened to mention that she had seen Julian at the airport. Apparently he was just getting out of a taxi as they were getting into one. She said that he didn't see them and...

'Anyway, I don't know why, but I just got a feeling that something wasn't quite right so I rang Julian. His telephone had been cut off and when I went round to his address his place was up to let. I tried his bank and all they would tell me was that they had no knowledge of his whereabouts. Brough's made some enquiries, though, and he's discovered that Julian has closed his account.

'No one seems to know where he's gone, Dee, or when he's coming back and I'm very much afraid...'

'That he won't *be* coming back,' Dee finished grimly for her.

'I think you're probably right, given what we know about his precarious finances. With fifty thousand pounds in his pocket he could quite easily have decided to cut his losses here, and dodge his debts, and simply

start the whole dishonest game afresh somewhere else.'
Anna bit her lip.

'Dee, I'm so sorry…'

'It's not your fault,' Dee assured her immediately. 'If
anyone's to blame, it has to be me.'

'What are we going to do?' Anna asked her anxiously.

'What *you* are going to do is relax and stop worrying,' Dee told her gently. 'As for what I shall do…I'm
not sure yet, Anna. God, but it makes me so angry to
think he's getting away with what he's done absolutely
scot-free. The man's only a hair's breadth away from
being a criminal, if indeed he isn't legally one, but it
isn't so much the actual money he's cheated other people out of that—'

Dee broke off and Anna could hear the emotion in
her husky voice as she continued shakily, 'It's the damage he's done to other people, the hurt and harm he's
caused.'

'Well, Beth seems to be recovering from her heartbreak over him now.' Anna tried to console her.

'Yes,' Dee agreed. 'But it isn't just—' She stopped
abruptly, and not for the first time Anna had the distinct
impression that there was much, much more to Dee's
determination to unmask Julian Cox than just the heartache he had caused Beth. She knew better than to pry,
though. Dee was an extremely proud woman, and a
rather vulnerable one behind that pride. If she wanted
to confide in her Anna knew that she would do so, and
until, or unless, she did so Anna felt that she had no
right to probe into what she guessed was an extremely
sensitive issue.

'Perhaps Dee and Julian were an item once,' Kelly
had once mused to Anna when they were discussing the

subject. 'Perhaps he dropped her in the same way he did Beth.'

But Anna had immediately shaken her head in denial.

'No. Never. Dee would never be attracted to a man like Julian,' she had told Kelly firmly. 'Never.'

'No. No, you're right,' Kelly had agreed. 'But there must be something.'

'If there is and if she wants to tell us about it then I'm sure she knows she can,' Anna had pointed out gently then, and a little shamefacedly Kelly had agreed that Dee was entitled to her privacy and her past.

'Dee, I feel so guilty about your money,' Anna repeated unhappily now. 'I should have realised... suspected...'

'There's no way I want you to feel guilty, Anna. In fact...'

Dee paused and then continued quietly, 'I rather suspected that something like this might happen, or I thought he might be tempted to try to abscond with the money. What I didn't allow for was that he would do it so openly or so fast. You aren't in any way to blame,' she added firmly. 'His situation must be even more desperate than I thought for him to have behaved so recklessly. After this there's no way he can come back, not to Rye. No way at all.

'What are you doing this weekend?' Dee asked, changing the subject.

'Nothing special. Beth's going down to Cornwall to see her parents. Kelly and Brough are away. What about you?'

'My aunt in Northumberland hasn't been too well again so I'm going to go up and see her. Her doctor wants her to have an operation but she's afraid that if she does she might not recover, so I thought I'd try to talk to her and make her see sense.'

'Dee, do you think we'll be able to track Julian down?'

'I'm not sure,' Dee told her soberly. 'If I know Julian he'll have gone somewhere where he can't be touched by European law and it probably isn't just *our* fifty thousand pounds he's taken with him.'

For a long time after she had said goodbye to Dee and replaced her telephone receiver, Anna stood silently in her conservatory, ignoring the indignant miaows of her cat, Whittaker, as he wove round her legs. Beth's mother, her cousin, had suggested that it was high time she paid a visit home to Cornwall. Perhaps she should, Anna acknowledged. The time was past now when the hurt of going back to the place she had once loved so much, knowing it had taken the life of the man she loved, had been too much for her to bear.

Their love had been a gentle, very young and idealistic kind of love, the intimacy between them a little awkward and hesitant, both of them learning the art of loving together, and what hurt more than anything else now was knowing that Ralph had never been allowed to reach his full potential, to grow from the boy he had in reality still been to the man he would have become.

She could barely remember now how it had felt to love him, how it had felt to be loved by him. Try as she might she could hardly conjure up now those nights they had lain in one another's arms. They seemed to belong to a different life, a different Anna.

No, there was no reason really why she shouldn't go back. She had forgiven the sea a long time ago for stealing her love. But had she forgiven herself for going on living without him?

She might not be able to recall his image very clearly any more but she could still vividly recall the look of anguish and resentment in his mother's eyes on the day of his funeral. It had told her, without the words being spoken, how bitterly his mother resented the fact that she was still alive whilst her beloved son was dead. How distressed, how guilt-ridden that look had made Anna feel. Now her guilt was caused by the fact that her memories of Ralph and their love were so distant that they might have belonged to someone else. She had loved him, yes, but it had been a girl's love for a boy. Now she was a woman, and if the vague but so sharply disturbing longings that sometimes woke her from her sleep were anything to go by she was increasingly becoming a woman whose body felt cheated of its rightful role, its capacity for pleasure, its need for love…

Anna drew in a distressed, sharp breath. She knew quite well that it was her ongoing training as a counsellor that was bringing to the fore all these unfamiliar and uncomfortable feelings, but that didn't make them any easier to bear.

Watching as Brough kissed his fiancée, Kelly, she had actually experienced the most shockingly sharp pang of envy. Not because Brough loved Kelly. That couldn't be the reason. Brough, much as she liked him, was simply not her type. No, her envy had been caused by the most basic feminine kind of awareness that her womanhood, her sexuality, was being deprived of expression.

But what did that mean? That she was turning into some kind of sex-starved middle-aged stereotype? Her body stiffened at the very thought, pride lifting her chin. That she most certainly was not. No way!

Her cat, seeing that his mistress wasn't going to respond to his overtures, stalked away in indignation. As she continued to stare out of the window Anna's soft blue-grey eyes misted a little.

At thirty-seven she still had the lithe, slender figure she had had at eighteen, and her hair was still as soft and silky, its honey-coloured warmth cut to shoulder-length now instead of worn halfway down her back. Ralph had used to run his fingers down its shiny length before he kissed her.

Anna gave a small, distraught shudder. What was the matter with her? She had met men, plenty of them—nice men, good men—in the years of her widowhood, and not once had she ever come anywhere near desiring any of them.

How irrational and unsolicited it was that her body should suddenly so keenly remember what desire was, how it felt, how it ached and urged, when her mind, her emotions, remained stubbornly resolute that they wanted no part in such a dangerous resurgence of her youthful sensuality.

'Yes. I'm sorry, I'm coming,' she acknowledged as Whittaker's protesting wails suddenly intruded on her thoughts.

CHAPTER THREE

HUMMING exultantly beneath his breath, Ward checked
the last signpost before his ultimate destination. Rye-
on-Averton.

It sounded such a middle England, respectable sort
of place, but at least one of its inhabitants was anything
but honest and trustworthy.

He hadn't been able to believe his luck when the
agents he had employed had informed him that, whilst
they could find no trace of Julian Cox, who according
to their enquiries had, in fact, left the country and apparently disappeared, his partner, Anna Trewayne, had
been traced to the small English town of Rye.

They had even been able to supply Ward with an
address and a telephone number, as well as a considerable amount of other pertinent information about Ms
Trewayne.

Widowed, childless, outwardly she appeared to live
a life of almost boring propriety and respectability.
Ward knew otherwise, of course. He could picture her
now. She was in her late thirties and no doubt struggling
to hold onto her youth. She probably possessed a certain
amount of surface charm—a useful tool for helping to
persuade vulnerable men to part with their money. Her
make-up would be too heavy and her skirts too short.
She would have sharp eyes and a keen interest in a
man's bank account and, of course, a very shrewd business brain—but not, it seemed, shrewd enough to warn
her to do what her erstwhile partner had done and dis-

appear whilst the going was good. Perhaps she even had
plans to continue with their 'business' on her own.

Perhaps he was a chauvinist but for some reason
Ward felt an even greater sense of revulsion and outrage
towards the woman who had cheated his half-brother
than he had done the man. An avaricious, heartless
woman. Ward had a deep sense of loathing for the
breed. His ex-wife had, after all, been one of them.

He dropped the speed of his powerful, top-of-the-
range Mercedes to turn off the bypass and into the town.

Nestled in a pretty green valley, it had an almost
picture-book quaintness. Mentally he compared it to the
grimy, run-down, inner-city area where he had grown
up and then grimaced. No haggard-faced, old-before-
their-time, out-of-work men gathered on the corners of
this place. No gangs of testosterone-driven youths with
nothing in front of them, no way out of the underclass
environment that trapped them, roamed these clean,
tree-lined streets.

Ward saw a parking area up ahead of him alongside
the river and he pulled into it. Time to study his map.
As he switched off the engine he was conscious of the
beginnings of a tension headache. He picked up the
street directory map he had brought with him. A few
seconds later Ward jabbed his forefinger triumphantly
onto the map as he found the place he was looking for.

Anna Trewayne lived a little way out of town, her
house solitary, without any neighbours, but then, no
doubt, a woman of her ilk would not want the complications that curious neighbours could bring.

As he reversed his car back into the traffic Ward's
expression was bleak.

Anna was in the garden when Ward arrived, the sound
of his car stopping on the gravel drive causing her to

put down the basket she had been filling with flowers
for the house and frown a little anxiously.

She wasn't expecting any visitors, and the car, like
the man emerging from it, was unfamiliar to her.

Expecting her visitor to announce himself at the front
door, Anna turned to slip into the house through the
still open conservatory door, but Ward just caught sight
of her flurried movement out of the corner of his eye
and, wheeling round, started to walk swiftly towards
her, calling out to her, 'Just a minute, if you please, Mrs
Trewayne; I want a word with you.'

Instinctively Anna panicked. Both the way he was
walking and the tone of his voice were distinctly threatening and she started to run towards the protection of
the conservatory, but she wasn't quite fast enough and
Ward caught up with her just as she reached the door,
grabbing hold of her wrist in a grip that almost made
her flinch at its strength.

'Let me go... I...I have a dog...' Anna told him,
issuing the first threat that came into her mind, but just
as she felt his grip starting to slacken Missie came trot-
ting round the corner, her small, furry body quivering
with welcome as she rushed happily towards Anna's
captor.

'So I see,' he agreed sardonically. He started to lift
his free hand and immediately Anna reacted, her fear
for her little dog far, far greater than her fear for herself.

'Don't you dare hurt her,' she told him fiercely, holding out her own free arm protectively to Missie.

The little dog, a bundle of white fluff, had been a
rescue dog, bought as a puppy and then abandoned
when the family who'd owned her had decided that her

small, sharp teeth were doing too much damage to their home.

Anna had taken her in, trained and loved her, and Missie adored her.

Ward frowned his surprise. Odd that a woman of her type should ignore her own danger just to protect her dog. Not that he had intended to hurt the little creature, and Missie seemed to know it.

Ignoring her mistress's frantic attempts to shoo her away, she was happily investigating the stranger's shoes, and then, as Ward extended his hand towards her, she jumped up and licked it, wagging her small tail approvingly.

'Look, I don't know who you are or what you want,' Anna began nervously, 'but—'

'But you *do* know Julian Cox, don't you?' Ward slipped in quietly.

'Julian.' Anna went pale. Was this man someone Julian had sent to demand more money from her? Had he perhaps guessed what they were doing?

As he watched the blood drain from her face Ward experienced a disturbingly unfamiliar—and unwanted—sensation. All right, she might not look anything like he had imagined. Her skirt was calf-length, all soft and floaty, and as for her make-up—well, she had to be wearing some, surely? No woman of her age could have such a soft, pink, kissable-looking mouth naturally, could she? And her hair had to be dyed, he decided triumphantly, whilst as for that air of frightened vulnerability she was projecting—well, that was, no doubt, as false as the colour of her hair.

'Don't bother lying to me,' Ward announced sternly. 'I know you know him and know something else as well. I know just what the pair of you have been up to…'

'The p-pair of us…?' Anna repeated, stammering a little. 'I…'

'I've got the evidence here,' Ward told her curtly, releasing Anna's wrist as he reached into the inside pocket of his suit.

As she rubbed her tender wrist Anna wished that she had the courage to risk slamming the conservatory door and locking him on the outside of it, but a quick, fleeting glance at him warned her of the danger of doing anything so reckless. For a start there was the size of him. He was…he was huge, she decided. So tall, over six feet, and so…so *big*. Not fat…no, not that. She could feel her face growing hot as her feminine instincts conveyed the message to her that the male body, under its quietly dignified suiting, owed its size to hard-packed male muscle and the kind of physique one might normally associate with a man who spent a lot of his time working physically hard. His hair was thick and dark brown, tinged unexpectedly with gold at the ends where the sun had caught it, giving him an almost leonine look.

'This *is* you, isn't it?' he demanded as he turned the paper he was holding towards Anna, jabbing his forefinger at a name printed on it.

Anna's eyes widened as she saw that it was her own.

'Yes. Yes…it is…' she admitted, her face burning hotly as she saw from the look he was giving her that he hadn't, after all, missed the discreet female inspection she had been giving him. Trying to ignore him, she forced herself to read the document. What on earth was it?

Anna blinked and stared hard at what he was holding,

her heart starting to pound heavily. In front of her on
the paper she could see her own name quite plainly, and
just as plainly beneath it was written the word 'partner.'
What on earth did it mean? Why on earth had Julian
Cox untruthfully and surely illegally claimed her as his
partner? Anna had no idea. All she could assume was
that he had done it because he'd felt it added weight
and credibility to whatever he had been planning. Or
had he perhaps known that something like this could
happen and, in that knowledge, had deliberately set her
up to act as a fall guy? Anna wondered queasily. He
was, she knew, perfectly capable of that kind of deliberately dishonest behaviour.

The words of denial and protest springing to her lips
were ruthlessly suppressed. Could this be the break-
through, the evidence of Julian's fraudulent deceit
which Dee had striven so hard to find? She needed time
to think, Anna decided, time to consult Dee and tell her
what had happened, and, most of all, she needed that
all-important piece of paper. But as she reached out to
take it, as though he sensed what she was about to do,
the man stepped back from her, determinedly folding it
and putting it back in his pocket.

'Well, your partner might have been clever enough
to disappear, but you, it seems, were less wise—or perhaps more arrogant,' Ward challenged softly.

Arrogant!

Anna couldn't believe what she was hearing.

'How does it feel, knowing that you have deprived
other people of their money; that this house, the clothes
you wear and the food you eat are, no doubt, paid for
out of other people's pockets?' Ward demanded with
scornful anger. 'Nothing to say?' he queried. 'No pro-
tests of innocence? You *do* surprise me.'

He would be even more surprised if he knew the truth, Anna reflected, but would he believe her if she tried to tell him? From the look on his face, somehow she doubted it. But if he thought she was going to stand there and allow him to revile her verbally...

Tilting her head so that she could look straight into his eyes, she told him firmly, 'Look, I'm sorry if you feel that you've been cheated...' She paused. Something about his attitude made her so angry that she felt physically weak at the knees. At least, she supposed it must be anger; after all, what else could it be?

She smiled sweetly before saying, very, very gently, 'However, surely the fact that you were being offered such an exceptionally high rate of interest on your investment must have alerted you to the fact that something might not be quite...genuine...?'

Ward could scarcely believe his ears. Was she actually daring to tell him that it was his *own* fault he had been cheated; that *he* had been guilty of either a lack of intelligent caution or an excess of simple greed?

Her head barely touched his shoulder. She was as fine-boned as a little bird and he guessed that he could have spanned her waist with both his hands and picked her up off the ground without straining his breath, and yet she stood there and had the audacity to challenge him!

Reluctantly Ward acknowledged that she had guts. Certainly more than her partner. By heaven, though, she was cool and calm—both virtues that he admired.

Abruptly he pulled himself back from the dangerous brink he was teetering on, reminding himself of just what she had done.

'I'm sure it would have,' he agreed grimly. 'I pride myself on being able to spot a phoney a mile off. As it happens it isn't me the pair of you gulled—but then, of course, you know that already.

'Does the name Ritchie Lewis mean anything to you?' he shot at Anna.

'No…I've never heard of him before,' Anna told him honestly, starting to frown as she questioned, 'But if you didn't invest money with Julian then what are you doing here?'

'Ritchie is my half-brother,' he told her impatiently, demanding bitingly, 'Have you any idea just what you've done? Ritchie should be studying, not worrying about the loss of five thousand pounds. No, of course you haven't,' he told her scornfully. 'I'll bet you've never strayed out of your cosseted, comfortable little world. Of course you don't know what it is to suffer pain, disappointment—'

'You're making judgements about me without know-ing the first thing about me,' Anna interrupted him swiftly, her gentle expression suddenly replaced by one of pride and anger.

'Oh, but I do know the first thing about you. I know that you're a liar and a cheat,' Ward returned softly.

Anna gave a sharp gasp.

'Well…nothing to say?' Ward demanded.

'I…I don't intend to say anything until…until I've spoken to my legal advisors,' Anna fibbed, suddenly gaining inspiration from a recent television series she had been watching.

'Your legal advisors? They're no doubt as guilty of sharp practice as you and your precious partner,' Ward told her bluntly. 'Well, let me tell you here and now, there's no way I'm going to let him or you get away with this. You owe my half-brother five thousand pounds and I intend to make sure you pay it back.'

'You do?' Anna was impressed. Dee would love to meet this man, she knew. Here at last was someone who was prepared to stand up to Julian; to pursue him, Anna was certain, to the furthermost corners of the earth with relentless determination.

Even so, there was something about his attitude towards *her* that had got her hackles rising in a way she could never remember anyone else doing.

'Er…what you have to say is extremely interesting, Mr…er…'

'Hunter,' Ward supplied briefly. 'Her— Ward Hunter.'

Ward Hunter. Well, at least now she had his name. She could pass it on to Dee along with the information he had given her and then she could leave him and Dee to pursue Julian Cox together.

Suddenly Anna had a brainwave.

'You say you want me to repay your half-brother's money. I'm afraid I don't have five thousand pounds here at home with me. Could you call back, say, tomorrow…?'

Ward stared at her. Now what was she up to? One minute she was claiming she knew nothing about the money, the next she was accusing him of deserving to be cheated, and now here she was calmly and coolly announcing that she would repay him. She was even more dangerous than Ward had first suspected.

'Why should I believe you? You could pull the same disappearing stunt as your partner.'

'Leave the country, you mean.' Anna looked down at where Missie was lying on the conservatory floor. 'No. I couldn't do that,' she said simply and ridiculously.

Ward found that he believed her. She might be quite

happy to cheat his brother and goodness knew how many others, but he had seen the love in her eyes when she looked at her dog. She wasn't going to abandon her.

'I could, of course, give you a cheque now,' Anna suggested sweetly. The look he gave her in return almost made her want to laugh.

'Which your bank would, no doubt, refuse to honour,' he told her, shaking his head. 'No, I don't think so. I want the cash…'

'Then you will just have to wait until tomorrow,' Anna told him firmly.

'Very well, then,' Ward agreed. 'I'll be here at nine sharp.'

'Nine? But the bank doesn't open until ten,' Anna protested.

'Exactly,' Ward responded smoothly. 'I can hardly allow you to take the risk of travelling there and back alone with such a large sum of money. I shall come with you.'

'Come with me…?' Anna's outrage momentarily overwhelmed her. 'Perhaps you'd like to stay the night and keep me chained to your side,' she said acidly, only to flush bright red as she saw the look in his eyes.

Ward was as startled by the bright pink glow of her cheeks as Anna was. It would have been much more in character for her to have deliberately flirted with him, to have flaunted her sexuality and drawn his attention to it rather than to betray such embarrassment. It was just another one of her tricks, of course, and one she had no doubt used to good effect in the past on the more vulnerable members of his sex. He could well imagine how easily a man might feel tempted to rush to protect and cherish her. She was so tiny, so fragile…and yet, at the same time, so determinedly and so ridiculously feisty.

Angrily he turned away from her, warning her as he did so, 'Don't even think of not being here because I promise you, wherever you go I shall find you.'

He had just started to walk back to his car when Missie suddenly darted out from behind Anna and ran after him, whining pathetically.

Immediately he stopped, turned round and dropped down to fuss the little dog. From his kneeling position he looked up at Anna and growled, 'Poor little thing. She deserves better—someone worthy of her loyalty and her trust, someone who knows what those things mean and values them, respects them.'

And then, before Anna could say a word, he got to his feet and strode towards his car.

Of all the nerve! What an arrogant, insensitive block-head of a man, Anna fumed once he had gone. Nursing Missie on her lap and chiding her for her treachery, she told the dog severely, 'Well, I certainly feel sorry for his wife.'

His wife. Heavens, but it must take an awful long time to caress every inch of that big hard chest, and heaven knew how much coaxing and cajoling it must take to get that hard mouth soft enough to kiss it. And as for his oh, so high moral principles... What must it be like to have to break through that stern, austere bar-rier to get him to react emotionally, to drive him out of control with longing and desire? If he were to wrap his arms around *her* she would be lost in them, Anna re-flected. It would be like being mauled by a lion. Was his body hair as soft and delicious to touch as her old teddy's? Did he growl, too, if you pressed his middle?

Anna gave a little giggle, her eyes dancing with

amusement. Oh, but there was so much of him. A woman would have to be either very brave or very foolish to risk falling in love with him. He had been so antagonistic towards her, so ready to believe the worst...and yet, at the same time...Sternly she reprimanded herself.

'Down you go. I need to ring Dee,' she told Missie, gently dislodging her from her lap.

Anna's heart sank when she listened to the message on Dee's answering machine. She had, she informed her callers, gone north to see her aunt.

Anna had the number of her mobile but when she tried it there was no reply. Well, she would just have to try again later, she decided. Heavens, but Ward Hunter had been so rude, so aggressive. She just hoped she had been right in thinking that paper he had could be used against Julian Cox. She certainly had never given Julian permission to name her as his partner, and his doing so had been a blatant piece of fraud on his part. Mulling over what she had learned, Anna headed for her kitchen.

She was an enthusiastic cook but she was the first to admit that there was much more fun in cooking for others than in cooking for herself, which was one of the reasons she enjoyed her work with the elderly so much. Which reminded her...

She would make herself something to eat and then she would go outside and finish her gardening before it got too dark.

Half an hour after leaving Anna, Ward was booking into a local hotel. It had been a warm day and he was beginning to feel in need of a shower and something to eat. After the porter had gone he looked a little disparagingly around the room. He had booked into the first hotel he had come across. Luxurious living was something Ward could either take or leave. He liked good things, appreciated them, and had a good eye for quality, but the comfort of a five-star hotel with a highly recommended restaurant was the last thing on his mind right now.

God, but she was the most distracting, deceitful, downright dangerous woman he had ever met.

When the sunlight had shone through that long skirt thing she had been wearing, revealing slim, surprisingly long legs, it had been all he could do to drag his gaze away.

It couldn't possibly have been deliberate, and neither could the way her soft stretch tee shirt top had clung to the warmly rounded outline of her breasts as she'd bent so protectively towards her ridiculous little dog.

Her bare arms had been softly pale, just barely sprinkled with pretty freckles, and Ward had had to fight an overwhelming urge to run his fingertip all the way up the soft flesh of one of them from her wrist right up past her breast. She had smelled distractingly of roses and honeysuckle and there had been a piece of clematis in her hair that he had itched to reach out and remove.

He had wanted to hold her, stroke her and shake her all at the same time, so confusing and conflicting had been his reactions to her.

One reaction had been uncompromisingly plain, though. His jaw tightened irritably. He was forty-two and he couldn't remember the last time his body had given such an impromptu display of its potent maleness.

Thankfully he had managed to control it before *she* had seen what was happening.

Ward swallowed hard. There was a print on the bedroom wall, a cornfield bright with red poppies, and, for
one logic-defying moment, he could almost breathe in
the field's summer scent, feel the itchy sharpness of it
against his bare skin, the sun hot against his naked body
as he wrapped Anna's equally naked form in his arms.
Her flesh felt so soft, her breasts delicious mounds of
femininity, creamily pale, throwing into prominence the
erotic, contrasting darkness of her nipples. He touched
them with his fingertips and heard her indrawn breath
of pleasure, saw the eager, wanton look in her eyes as
she commanded him, 'Kiss them, Ward. I want to feel
you mouth against me.'

Ward closed his eyes. The little triangle of hair between her thighs felt so unbelievably silky soft.

'Ward, I want you so much...' he heard her whisper.

Ward opened his eyes. Damn her. What *was* she,
some kind of witch? Well, she wasn't going to bewitch
him. *No way*. His body felt hot and tense, aching with
angry desire. Very deliberately he ran the shower cold.
That should put a damper on such dangerous thoughts,
amongst other things!

That was all the dead-heading done. Now all she needed
to do was to put everything away and then she could
go and have a bath. Heavens, she was tired. Her whole
body ached. A little guiltily Anna flushed. It wasn't just
the gardening she had been doing that was causing that
ache. Now, where was that hoe she had been using—a
long-handled one especially useful for recalcitrant
weeds? Tiredly Anna stepped backwards, and then cried
out in pain as she inadvertently trod on the hoe and the
handle came up and hit her right on the back of
her head.

*   *   *

Missie whined unhappily. Why was her mistress lying in the middle of the lawn ignoring Missie's anxious little cries and licks...?

Ward pushed away the room-service meal he had ordered, half-eaten. It was no good. He simply didn't trust that woman. By morning she could be heaven alone knew where. Quickly Ward gathered up his coat and his keys, almost running out of the hotel towards his car.

Missie greeted his arrival with excited, relieved little barks. Ward frowned. The house was in complete darkness, even though it was now dusk, and the conservatory door was open. Where the devil was Anna?

Missie showed him, standing anxiously beside her unconscious mistress, her little tail beating the ground as she looked trustingly up at Ward.

On the ground Anna gave a little moan and started to open her eyes.

'Oh, my head hurts,' she cried out, tears filling her eyes.

'It's all right; you've bumped it. Don't move. I'm going to call for an ambulance,' Ward told her grimly.

When Anna had moved her head he had seen the dark patch of drying blood staining her hair and he could see a smear of blood on the handle of the hoe, too.

'Who are you?' he heard Anna asking him fretfully.

He checked before he started to dial the emergency services number on his mobile phone and stared at her.

'Don't you know?' he asked her.

Tearfully Anna looked at him.

'No, I don't.' She started to shiver as she told him frantically, 'I don't know anything.'

Without answering her Ward quickly dialled 999.

* * *

'She seems to have lost her memory,' he told the para-
medic some fifteen minutes later after they had carefully
lifted Anna into the ambulance and out of earshot.

'It can happen,' he told Ward. 'She could be concussed. We'll know more once we've done some proper
tests. I take it you weren't with her when it happened?'

'No…No, I wasn't…' Ward agreed.

'You say her name's Anna Trewayne, and you're…?'

'Ward Hunter,' Ward supplied.

'So you're not married.' The other man gave a brief,
dismissive shrug. 'If you'd like to follow us to the hospital in your car, I'm sure the consultant will want to
talk with you.'

'But I'm not…' Ward began, but the man was already jumping into the ambulance and it had started to
pull away.

After bundling Missie into his own car and closing
the conservatory door, Ward followed it. After all, what
else *could* he do with Missie looking so imploringly at
him?

'If you'd just wait here, Mr Hunter, the consultant will
be along to see you in a moment.'

Anna had been whisked away on a stretcher the minute they had entered the hospital's casualty department,
and now, so far as Ward could glean from the busy desk
in the foyer area, the consultant had finished examining
her and she was in a bed on one of the wards.

'Mr Hunter?'

Nodding, Ward held out his hand to the consultant.

'How is she?' he asked without preamble as the other
man ushered him into a small cubicle off the main foyer
area.

'Well, so far as we can ascertain she hasn't sustained

any serious damage. There's a considerable amount of bruising and some external bleeding, but fortunately there aren't any signs of internal bleeding. We'll want to keep a check on her for the next few weeks, but that can be done via her GP.'

The consultant glanced at his watch and frowned. He should have been off duty three hours ago but an unexpected emergency had kept him at the hospital, which was how he had come to be there to examine Anna.

'She's regained consciousness fully now and since there aren't any obvious problems we can discharge her and let her go home.'

'On her own?' Ward queried. He suspected that, like many others, the hospital might be short of beds and, although he knew the consultant would never have discharged Anna if he wasn't confident that it was medically safe to do so, Ward certainly did not feel, judging from what he had seen, that she would be anywhere near strong enough yet to cope by herself.

The consultant's eyebrows rose, his voice suddenly a few degrees cooler as he heard the criticism in Ward's voice.

'I take it you *will* be there with her?' he responded.

Him?

Ward was just about to deny any such thing when the consultant continued carefully, 'Of course, there is this added problem of her temporary loss of memory— it's a complication which does occur sometimes with head injuries. Fortunately, in our experience, the patient's full memory eventually returns in almost one hundred per cent of cases. In Anna's case, it just seems to be her recent memories she isn't able to recall. She knows her name and her family background, for instance, but she was unable to tell us what she had done

today or who she had seen; the last memory she seems
to recall is over several months ago.'

'She's lost her memory?' Ward started to frown, and
the words 'and you're sending her home' trembled on
his lips, but he controlled himself long enough to suppress them. Had Anna been a member of his own family, right now he would have been ruthlessly bypassing
the harried man in front of him and insisting not just
on a second opinion but on Anna being referred to a
private hospital.

Anna, though, was not a member of his family. Anna
was *nothing* whatsoever to do with him—apart from the
fact that she owed him five thousand pounds.

'Of course, if she should start to complain of suffering any kind of head pains, double vision, sickness, that
kind of thing, then bring her straight back in.'

'If she should... Is she *likely* to?' Ward demanded
tersely.

'Not so far as I am able to judge,' the consultant
assured him.

'And you say that she will regain her memory...'

'I should think so. Although, of course, I can't say
when. Sometimes patients experience a flashback and
total recall; other times their memory returns in stages.'

The consultant's bleeper started to go off. He was
already turning away, his body language indicating that
he was a busy man.

Damn, Ward cursed under his breath as he watched
him hurry down the corridor. *Now* what was he supposed to do? Realistically he owed Anna nothing. Quite
the opposite. And he had a perfect right to walk out of
the hospital and leave her to sort out her own problems.
Realistically, perhaps, but what about morally...?

Morally...

What about *her* moral obligations to his half-brother and the others she had cheated?

So she was a liar and a cheat; did that mean he had to descend to the same level of callousness? Ward asked himself quietly. He might not want to help her but it simply went against his whole character for him to walk off and leave her in her present condition.

'Mr Hunter?' a nurse enquired, coming up to him. 'The consultant has already informed Anna that she can go home. She's just getting dressed, so if you'd like to come with me...'

As he turned to follow the nurse onto the ward, a sudden thought struck Ward—a possible escape route from the unwanted chore of taking charge of Anna until she either regained her memory or someone more appropriate turned up to take over from him.

Stopping abruptly, he asked the nurse curtly, 'This amnesia—I don't suppose it could be...imaginary...could it?'

'Imaginary amnesia?' The nurse gave him a sharp look. 'Sometimes we *do* have patients who fake memory loss for one reason or another, but our consultant here would soon detect any sign of *that* in a patient. Why do you ask?' she questioned him curiously. 'Do you have some reason to suppose that Anna is faking her amnesia? Occasionally we have patients who have suffered such intense trauma that their only possible escape route is to pretend that it has never happened, but in Anna's case...'

'No. No...' Ward hastened to reassure her. Good grief, the next thing he knew the nurse would probably be accusing him of causing Anna's trauma.

'I can assure you, Mr Hunter,' the nurse said tartly, 'that if Anna has been diagnosed by our Mr Bannerman as suffering from temporary amnesia, then temporary amnesia is *exactly* what she *is* suffering from.'

They had reached the entrance to the ward now and Ward could see Anna standing forlornly beside her bed, her expression anxious and strained.

No matter what she might have done, Ward couldn't help feeling a small surge of compassion for her. To be unable to remember even the most basic detail of one's current life was not a position he would want to be in.

Anna's eyes lit up as she saw the nurse. Obviously she recognised *her*, Ward decided, and then he realised with a sharp frisson of unfamiliar emotion that it was *him* she was looking at, not the nurse.

'Ward?' She said his name uncertainly and tremulously, her eyes more grey than blue and stomach-achingly haunted.

'You recognise me?' he demanded, ignoring the small, disapproving shake of her head the nurse was giving him.

Immediately Anna's mouth trembled betrayingly.

'No, I don't.' She shook her head. 'But Nurse James told me your name. She said I could go home,' she added, her eyes brightening and then darkening again at this thought.

The nurse had slipped diplomatically away, leaving them alone together.

'I...I'm sorry I don't remember you,' Ward heard Anna telling him softly, biting her lip before continuing in a small rush, 'But in a way I do. I can sense...feel that...that there's something very special between us...'

She started to flush a little, her glance meeting Ward's and then sliding away almost shyly.

'You can sense that?' Ward queried, his voice suddenly disconcertingly gruff when he had intended it to sound sarcastic.

'Yes. Yes, I can,' Anna confirmed. And then, to Ward's bemusement, she reached out and touched his face very gently with her fingertips, the look on her face one of tender joy.

'I know that I can't recognise or remember you at the moment, Ward, and I can understand how hard that must be for you. I know how concerned you are about me.'

A pair of dimples suddenly appeared at either side of her mouth as she smiled teasingly at him.

'The consultant told me how you'd interrogated him about me...'

God, but she looked so heart-achingly vulnerable. The trust in her eyes, in her touch, made Ward's throat close up. He shuddered to think of the appalling and dangerous situation she could have found herself in with someone less honourable than himself.

'I'm so glad you're here with me, Ward,' Anna confided. 'It feels so odd not being able to remember...so frightening. Mr Bannerman told me that you aren't my husband...'

'No,' Ward agreed shortly.

'But we *are* partners. He said you'd told the ambulance staff that,' Anna continued.

Ward ground his teeth. He had told them no such damned thing. *They* had made the assumption that he and Anna were a pair, because their laughable urgency in getting her to hospital had not given him any opportunity to correct their misinterpretation of his presence at her house.

'How much exactly can you remember?' he demanded brusquely.

Uncertainly Anna stepped back from him, her hand dropping away. Ridiculously he felt oddly bereft, as though a part of him had actually enjoyed having her touch him.

'Everything, and then nothing since some time early this year.' Anna gave him a painful smile. 'I can't remember how we met or when, how long we've been together.'

Her eyes filled with tears which she immediately tried to blink away, her fingers twisting her wedding ring in agitation.

'Well, don't worry about it,' Ward told her, trying to comfort her. 'The consultant says you'll get your memory back fully eventually. Come on, let's get you home,' he added, starting to guide her towards the door, but, to his consternation, instead of preserving the small distance he had placed between them, Anna closed it, snuggling up to his side and slipping her arm through his.

'Home. Well, at least I know where that is.' She stopped, her face shadowing again. 'Where do *we* live, Ward? I can't remember.' Ward could see the panic darkening her eyes. 'I know where *my* house is, but...'

'That's where we're going,' Ward told her.

What the hell was he doing? Ward asked himself as he guided her out to his car. Why the *hell* hadn't he simply told the consultant the truth? Now just look at the situation he had got himself into. Anna quite plainly thought they were lovers, which was ironic when he thought of the real relationship between them, and that was bad enough. How the hell he was going to manage to fabricate answers for the questions she was bound to ask him he had absolutely no idea.

When he had given in to his chivalrous, protective

male instinct and the moral code instilled in him by his mother and his stepfather, he hadn't realised the complications it was going to cause. But what was taxing him even more than that was the apparent total change in Anna's character. Did bumps on the head and amnesia do that? Could she have changed at a blow from an avaricious, self-seeking, heartless flirt, who preyed on the innocent and unaware, into this gentle, vulnerable, tender-eyed woman who made no pretence of being anything other than thoroughly relieved to be able to lean on him?

He had heard that blows to the head could cause bizarre behavioural changes, but not, surely, quite like this?

It was one o'clock in the morning now. Ward had, to say the least, had a challenging day, and right now he simply didn't have the energy to pursue the issue.

Ultimately, of course, he was going to have to tell Anna the truth—if she didn't regain her memory in the next few days he would have no option but to do so— once he had tracked down someone close to her who could take responsibility for her, of course. There was no way he could simply walk out and leave her in her present condition. And, of course, whilst he stayed close to her there was no way she was going to be able to disappear without repaying Ritchie's five thousand pounds.

'Oh, *this* is your car!' Anna exclaimed in obvious surprise as they reached the Mercedes and Ward unlocked it. Ward frowned. Why was she so surprised? It was an expensive car, yes, but then, to judge from what he had seen of her home, her own living standards must be reasonably comfortable, and from what he knew of her lifestyle she was surely not the type of woman who would be unfamiliar with things such as luxury cars. Far from it, he would have suspected.

Suddenly Anna saw the little dog curled up on the back seat of the car and immediately her face broke into a delighted smile.

'Oh, Missie,' she breathed.

'You recognise her,' Ward commented unnecessarily.

'Oh, yes,' Anna confirmed. 'I got her last year; she'd been abandoned and...' She paused. 'I know she's mine, Ward, but *when* was last year? I...'

To Ward's consternation her eyes filled with tears again.

'It's all right, you *will* remember.' He tried to reassure her, opening the passenger door of the car and urging her towards it, but Anna had other ideas. Ward was totally unprepared when she turned to *him* instead of the car and buried her head against his shoulder. She whispered, 'Hold me, Ward—oh, please, just hold me...I'm so frightened.'

Uneasily Ward hesitated. *This* wasn't something he had taken into account at all. He was, generally speaking, a man who prided himself on keeping his head in any kind of crisis—or at least he had been—but there was something about the soft warmth of Anna pressed so trustingly against him that caused the normal logical thought processes of his brain to be thrown into complete disarray.

'It's all right, don't worry, I'm here...'

Even as he heard himself saying the words, Ward knew that he had crossed a fateful Rubicon, but he told himself he was far too practical a person to listen to the unfamiliar inner voice warning him of danger.

How, after all, could *he* be in any possible danger? He knew exactly what kind of woman Anna really was and when she got her memory back she would be throwing him out, not *herself* into his arms.

Her hair smelled of roses and Ward could feel her trembling slightly as he held her.

Instinctively he lifted his hand to her hair to stroke it and then dropped it again.

'I think perhaps we haven't been together all that long,' Anna told him several seconds later, half laughing and half embarrassed as she moved away from him. In the illuminated car park Ward could see that her face was prettily flushed and that she looked both amused and self-conscious, her mouth curving into a slightly rueful smile.

She told him, 'That's what my body says, anyway, judging by the way I'm reacting to you. I don't think I'd still be trembling in your arms quite so—so intensely if we were long-time lovers.'

Trembling in his arms. Ward closed his eyes and swallowed—hard.

'We did meet only recently,' he admitted a little hoarsely as he helped her into the car.

It was, after all, the truth. He just hoped she wouldn't ask him how recent 'recently' actually was, but fortunately, when he got into the driver's seat, she was too busy hugging Missie to ask him any more questions.

As he drove Anna home, Ward's mind was busy. He would have to call at the hotel tomorrow and pay his bill. But what about his clothes? He hadn't known how long he would need to be in Rye so he had packed a suitcase, but there was hardly enough in it if he was supposed to be living with Anna; he would need rather more than what he had.

And then there was his own life. Fortunately he had his laptop with him, and even more fortunately there

was no one in his life who was likely to question his
absence. He would have to ring Mrs Jarvis, though, his
twice-weekly cleaner, to warn her that he wasn't going
to return home for a while.

Anna closed her eyes and leaned her head back against
the head-rest.

It felt so odd not being able to remember properly.
She knew who she was and where she came from; she
could remember quite clearly her family, her friends,
her way of life here in Rye and the tragedy which had
originally brought her here. But meeting Ward, their life
together, the events of the last few months and even
Ward himself—these were all things of which she had
no memory whatsoever.

The consultant had explained to her that she had suffered a blow to her head through standing on a garden
hoe.

'You were concussed, and although there was what
looked like a lot of blood fortunately no real damage
was done.'

'Apart from the memory,' Anna had reminded him.

'Apart from that,' he had agreed. 'Try not to worry
too much about it. It *will* return.'

'But when?' Anna had asked him anxiously.

'I'm afraid that's impossible to say,' he had told her.

'Will I…will I have to stay here in hospital?' Anna
had asked him anxiously.

'No,' he had assured her. 'Although if there wasn't
someone at home to look after you it would be different.'

Someone at home. Ward. The man who had brought
her here to the hospital.

Anna felt oddly breathless and dizzy just thinking

about him, her heart starting to race. He was so big, so masculine. Her skin started to heat as she realised the direction her thoughts were taking. Heavens, surely a woman of her age shouldn't get so giddily excited just thinking about her partner…her lover…

Ward… So familiar to her in some ways—she had immediately felt at home in his arms, recognised his scent, his feel—and yet a complete stranger to her in so many others. She was going to have to learn all about him all over again. Where had they met and when? Did he have a family? Had he ever been married? Did he have children?

Tomorrow she would ask him, Anna decided tiredly as Ward swung his car between the gates to her house.

At least she could recognise and remember that! She had no idea why Ward was living with her here. Why had she and Ward decided that they should live in *her* house? They must have had a reason—but she had to admit that she was pleased that they were living here. Having to contend with a house she couldn't even remember would have been far too daunting a prospect right now.

CHAPTER FOUR

'YOU sit down; I'll put the kettle on and make us both a drink.'

'No, Ward, let me do it,' Anna insisted. They were both in her kitchen, Missie tucked up happily in her basket whilst, next to her, the huge cream and brown cat, Whittaker, stretched languidly in his.

On the point of insisting that she needed to rest, Ward suddenly remembered that he would be expected to know his way around Anna's kitchen *and* the rest of her house.

'Well, if you're sure you'll be okay,' he agreed. 'I'll just get your stuff out of the car and take it upstairs.'

Anna had refused to put the blood-stained jacket she had been wearing back on and the hospital had also supplied her with some ointment to put on the broken skin of her scalp. On the pretext of disposing of them he could have a brief look round the upstairs of the house and familiarise himself with its layout, Ward decided.

In the morning before Anna woke up he would also have to slip out to the hotel, but that was a problem he could worry about then.

He had collected everything from the car and was halfway upstairs when he heard Anna calling out urgently to him. Dropping her jacket and the ointment, he rushed back to the kitchen.

'What is it?' he demanded abruptly. 'Are you ill? Do you feel sick? Are your eyes—?'

'Oh, Ward, I'm sorry…it's nothing like that,' Anna assured him remorsefully. 'I just wanted to know how you like your coffee…I'm afraid I can't remember…'

'Strong, black, no sugar,' Ward told her curtly.

Hell, for a moment he had feared…He closed his eyes and then flinched in shock as he felt Anna's lips brush his jaw.

'Thank you,' he heard her whisper tenderly.

She was thanking him?

'For what?' he asked her almost brusquely, opening his eyes and moving back from her, determinedly avoiding her, turning his head to look into those oh, so dangerous blue-grey eyes.

'For being here…for caring…for being you,' Anna told him softly.

The look in her eyes, so trusting, so…so giving…made Ward gulp.

It just wasn't possible that a simple blow on the head could so totally transform a person's personality—was it?

'Oh, I'm sorry,' Anna said, sleepily stifling a second yawn. They had finished their coffee and Ward had insisted that she was to stay where she was, sitting at the table, whilst he cleared up.

Although she lived alone, Anna's house was a comfortable size. She came from a large extended family and when Beth and Kelly had first moved to Rye she had been only too delighted to put them up. Her house had four good-sized bedrooms and her own large bedroom had its own separate bathroom.

Downstairs, in addition to the large kitchen with its pretty dining conservatory which she had added, there was a more formal dining room, a pretty sitting room

and a drawing room. Too much, perhaps, for one person, and certainly far larger than the pretty little cottage
she and Ralph had started married life in.

She had bought the house with some of the money
she had received from Ralph's life insurance policies—
the rest of the money, quite a considerable sum, had
been invested. She had been upset at first at the thought
of touching it, had even suggested that it ought more
properly to go to Ralph's parents, but both her own and
Ralph's family were comfortably off and, in the end,
she had listened to them and had accepted that they
were probably right in saying that Ralph would have
wanted her to have the money. Although Anna suspected that neither of Ralph's parents, especially his
mother, would ever feel totally comfortable in her presence because of the memories she brought back, both
of them had been genuinely determined that the pro-
ceeds of the insurance policy Ralph had taken out when
they married should go to Anna.

It was a mother's love for her child that caused
Ralph's mother to be so anguished whenever she saw
Anna, not the money, and Anna, always so sensitive,
could appreciate just how she must feel, just how she
herself might feel in the same circumstances.

Her own father was an architect and until Ralph's
death she had worked for him as his personal assistant.
He had understood why she had felt she had to leave
Cornwall, even though he had told her how much he
was going to miss her quiet efficiency.

The house was decorated with the same quiet good
taste exhibited by her clothes and her whole way of life,
and Ward, who was still trying to come to terms with
the powerful surge of desire he had felt earlier on when

she had touched him, couldn't help contrasting her manner with his ex-wife's.

She had never, so far as he could recall, voluntarily reached out to him in the way that Anna had just done, and when he had tried to bring a little tenderness into their relationship she had pushed him away, declaring, 'Don't be so soft.'

Soft. Him. Well, he might have been then, but he certainly wasn't any more. And he most definitely wasn't soft enough to forget just exactly what kind of woman Anna Trewayne really was.

'You're tired,' he told her shortly as she stifled another yawn. 'Why don't you go to bed?'

'What about you?' Anna asked him uncertainly.

'I'll be up later,' Ward told her, deliberately turning away from her so that she couldn't see his face.

It was so obvious that Anna assumed they would be sharing a bed, and just as obvious that there was no way he could allow that to happen. For one thing…well, he lived alone and normally slept in the raw, and he was used to having the whole of his large king-sized bed to himself. If he rolled over in his sleep, Anna, tiny little thing that she was… And besides— But he didn't want to allow himself to think the highly personal and explosively dangerous thoughts that were crowding his brain—thoughts which were of a far, far too intimate and sensual nature.

He heard Anna's chair scrape over the floor as she got up. Even with his back turned he knew that she was walking towards him.

'Good—goodnight, then,' he heard her saying a little breathlessly. Automatically he turned round. Anna was smiling tremulously up at him, lifting her face, her *mouth* towards his, plainly expecting to be kissed.

Who the hell was he trying to kid? Ward asked himself angrily. *This* was the reason why he didn't want to share a bed with Anna... The harshly guttural sound of protest he had been about to make was lost as he wrapped his arms around her and bent his mouth to hers.

'Mmm... Oh, yes...' Anna breathed delightedly as she wriggled closer to him. 'Oh, yes... Oh, Ward!' Blissfully she leaned into him. How could she possibly have forgotten *this*? She could feel her whole body reacting to Ward's kiss, right down to her toes which were curling sensuously into her shoes.

Experimentally she caressed his bottom lip with her tonguetip, her own body trembling with excitement as she felt him shudder. She suddenly felt like someone who had discovered undreamed-of treasure. Ralph, love him though she had, had *never* made her feel like this, but she felt no guilt. The relationship she had with Ward had already passed through those turbulent, traumatic waters, such feelings obviously resolved before they— *she*—had committed themselves to one another as lovers.

Anna might not be able to remember how or when they had met, or the nature of their courtship, but she knew herself and she knew just how powerful her feelings, her *love* must be for her to have become so intimate with him.

She must have experienced this rapture, this intensity, this total compulsion to abandon herself to him sexually and emotionally with him before, many times, but right now she couldn't recall those times, which must be why what she was feeling was so headily thrilling and exciting. She wanted desperately to touch him.

Touch him? She practically wanted to tear his clothes

off, she acknowledged ruefully, but he was already lifting his mouth from hers, his voice satisfactorily strained with emotion and desire as he told her thickly, 'The consultant said you had to rest...'

'Did he? I don't remember,' Anna teased him mischievously, but she still obediently let him go and started to make her way out of the kitchen, pausing only to fuss Missie and Whittaker.

Ward didn't dare to allow himself to relax until he was sure she had gone.

He couldn't remember the last time he had felt like this.

No, he didn't think he had *ever* felt like this. She had caught him off guard, that was all, he assured himself, and he'd have had to be made of stone not to respond to her. She was, after all, an extremely attractive woman, an extremely *sensual* woman—an extremely sexually experienced woman?

She had been instantly responsive to him, her body language making it plain just how much she wanted him, but earlier on this afternoon, despite what he knew about her, he had somehow gained the impression that she was not someone who was sexually promiscuous. There had been an innate feminine fastidiousness about her, a delicate hint of determined hauteur. And yet just now in his arms...

It had been all he could do not to show her just what she was doing to him, and there had even been a moment when, if he hadn't let her go, the urgency and intensity of his desire for her would have had him practically tearing the clothes off her—and that was something he had most certainly never come anywhere near wanting to do...ever...with any woman...

When he had met his ex-wife he had been full of

romantic ideals. He had put her up on something of a pedestal, respecting her. The thought of making love with her had made him go dizzy with longing, but when it had eventually happened, physically satisfying though the experience had been, emotionally it had been lacking in something.

He had told himself that the fault lay with him in that his expectations were too idealistic and unrealistic. Five minutes ago, holding Anna in his arms, he had discovered that they weren't.

Upstairs, in her bedroom, Anna undressed quickly. She wanted to be showered, all clean and sweetly scented, when Ward came to her.

This might not be their first time, but it would be the first of the *new* memories she would make with him and she wanted it to be very special. Not just for herself, but for Ward as well. She must have given him such a dreadful fright.

In her bathroom she had found a serviceable cotton robe and beneath her pillow there was an equally serviceable cotton nightdress. Frowningly she studied them. Surely she didn't wear *these* when she was with Ward?

Quickly she checked her drawers. It was odd how she knew automatically which ones held her underwear. It was all as dismally plain as her nightwear. Puzzled, she checked again. Instinctively she knew that for Ward she would have wanted to wear the most deliciously feminine things she could find, silky satin wisps of delicately coloured fabric, lavishly trimmed with lace, nothing vulgar or too provocative—she knew she wasn't the type for that—but surely, during the course of knowing him, she must have bought *something* to tease and tempt him with? If so, it certainly wasn't here.

Disappointed, she went back to the bed and climbed in. Well, if it was a choice of wearing that boring cotton nightdress or nothing, she'd take the nothing, thank you very much!

How long would Ward be? Not long, surely? A tiny shiver of nervous excitement ran through her. She felt almost like an old-fashioned virginal bride, madly in love with her husband, but also, at the same time, a little apprehensive about the intimacies that lay ahead.

Downstairs Ward waited half an hour and then another half an hour. The house was silent. Anna must surely be asleep by now?

Very quietly he crept upstairs. Her bedroom door was half open; he could see her lying to one side of the bed, thankfully asleep. She looked oddly forlorn and alone.

His mouth dry, Ward hurried past, pushing open the door to the bedroom furthest away from Anna's.

He had a quick shower, but no shave—his razor was still at the hotel, of course. If, in the morning, Anna questioned his desire to sleep in a different room he would tell her that the consultant had advised it—make up some story about him suggesting that it might be an idea for the two of them to put their intimate life on hold until Anna had recovered her memory.

Tiredly, Ward climbed into bed.

Anna woke up abruptly; her heart was pounding very fast and she was trembling. She had been having a frightening dream, but what about she could not remember. Her head ached a little and, whilst the nightmare fear had left her now, another much sharper fear had taken its place. What if she *never* recovered her memory? What if…?

'Ward. Ward?' She turned anxiously to the other side of the bed, only to discover that Ward wasn't there.

Thoroughly agitated, Anna pushed back the bedcovers. Where was he? She hurried out onto the landing. Whittaker, the cat, was just about to make his way into the end bedroom through the open door.

'Oh, no, you don't,' she chided him, padding after him and scooping him up. He was forbidden to sleep on the beds and well he knew it—but Whittaker's naughtiness was forgotten as she glanced into the room and realised that Ward was asleep in the bed.

What on earth was he doing in here? Bemused, but thoroughly relieved to have found him, Anna put the cat down and hurried over to the bed. He must be exhausted, poor man. She wouldn't wake him. Instead she slipped in beside him, cuddling as close to the warmth of his body as she could.

Mmm…he felt so good. *She* felt so good, so safe, so loved…so happy….

'Mmm…' Ward turned over in his sleep, his body instinctively accommodating the slight curve of Anna's, his arm curling round her, his leg, with genetically programmed male possessiveness and protection, moving to pin her gently to his side.

Happily Anna snuggled even closer. She wasn't quite asleep and the temptation to press a soft, delicate kiss against the muzzy warmth of his chest proved irresistible, and so too did the temptation to stroke her fingers through the soft mat of body hair tangled there.

'Just like a teddy bear', she marvelled softly under her breath, and then frowned. The words held a familiar echo, a vague ethereal recollection, but the harder she tried to grasp it, the fainter it became. Her agitation had woken Ward, though; she could feel his fingers tensing on her upper arm.

'Oh, Ward, you feel so good,' she whispered happily to him. 'Kiss me,' she begged him huskily.

Abruptly Ward became fully awake. What on earth was Anna doing in bed with him?

'Anna…' he began, but Anna had grown impatient of waiting for him to obey her command and she was already pressing her soft mouth against his, her lips warm and tender, clinging to his as her tonguetip traced their shape.

'Oh, Ward, I can't believe this is real,' she told him ecstatically. 'I'm just so lucky.'

He could feel her breasts pressing against his bare chest, her nipples provocatively hard. To his own horror Ward felt his hand lifting to cup one of them and caress it. Beneath her breath Anna gave a small, sucked-in sigh of pleasure and Ward felt her body start to arch against his own. Shockingly she was as naked as he was himself, her only covering the soft, silky triangle of body hair which right now was pressed tormentingly against his body. She was still kissing him, holding his face in her hands to keep him still as she pressed eager little kisses against his mouth.

Oh, God, he wasn't going to be able to stand much more of this; his body was already…

Ward gave an anguished groan as Anna, plainly aware of his arousal, moved her own body with simple directness to accommodate it.

That was *it*… It was no good, no *use* trying to pretend that he didn't want her, no use either trying to control that wanting when she was doing everything she could to encourage it. Ward almost cried out aloud as he felt her lift her hips so that she could press herself even more closely against him.

'Ward...' she whispered against his mouth.

Helplessly Ward felt himself succumb.

She felt too tiny, too fragile, to roll underneath him. He was afraid he might hurt her, so instead he moved the other way, lifting her with him so that she was lying on top of his body, their mouths still locked eagerly together.

Unable to stop himself, Ward ran his hands down the length of her body, cupping the delicious mounds of her buttocks, pressing her even deeper into his own flesh.

Anna moved wildly against him.

This was heaven, wonderful, unbelievable; her whole body was sighing with pleasure and love. Ward's hands swept round the front of her body and cupped her breasts.

They felt so heavy, taut with their need to be kissed and caressed. Almost as though he knew how she felt Ward urged her towards him, licking the swollen areolae that surrounded them, first one and then the other until Anna was wild with pleasure, trembling from head to foot, lost in the ecstasy of what she was feeling.

'Oh, yes, Ward, do that...do *that*,' she encouraged him throatily as he started to kiss each nipple, the sensation radiating through her body like nothing she could ever remember experiencing, but of course she *must* have experienced it before.

He could feel her stomach muscles tensing, locking, her pelvis lifting, and a sensation that came from lower, deeper within it, starting to grow and pulse out a rhythm that she instinctively began to respond to, her whole body moving against Ward's in time to it.

Ward knew he had totally lost control. There he was,

forty-two years old, and for the first time in his life he knew what it was to experience total abandonment and compelling, urgent desire. He wanted to possess Anna, absorb her completely into himself, devour her. Lost in the sensation that suckling on her nipples was giving him, he heard her cry out as his teeth accidentally grated against her sensitive flesh. Cursing himself, he stopped immediately, but as he started to release her Anna held him where he was.

'No. Don't stop,' she told him passionately. When Ward looked into them her eyes weren't grey any more but blue—the richest, hottest blue he had ever seen in his life. He groaned and reached out for her, cupping her face and drawing her down against him so that he could kiss her mouth.

Whilst he was doing so Anna moved eagerly against him and did what she had been aching to do ever since she had looked down the hospital ward and seen him walking towards her. As he felt her gentle fingers taking hold of him Ward closed his eyes. A small sob of sharp pleasure clogged his throat. He knew he should draw away, stop her, but he also knew that there was no way he was going to. There was something so unbearably erotic about having her guide his body into her own, something so heart-rockingly sweet about the absorbed expression on her face as she did so that his will-power just melted. She felt so good—hot, wet, her flesh surrounding his.

Anna gave a small moan of exquisite pleasure. It felt so good having Ward inside her. She moved experimentally against him and then caught her breath as he responded to her tentative movement. Wide-eyed, she focused on him, watching as he reached out and took hold of her, his hands just below her waist. Now it was

his turn to take control, to set the pace of their lovemaking, to move *her* to the rhythm of *his* desire, and
Anna couldn't believe how much she loved him doing
so, how much she revelled in the fiercely sweet pangs
of pleasure she could feel with each movement of his
body inside her. Slow at first, slow and careful, and then
harder and deeper and then deeper still, until...

'Ward. Ward...' Anna sobbed his name as she
reached her climax and felt the release of Ward's body
within hers, the hot, powerful surge of it leaving her
dizzy with feminine smugness and satisfaction. Exhausted, she leaned her head on his chest and closed
her eyes in mute happiness as she felt his arms close
around her.

What on earth had he *done*? Ward berated himself furiously as he automatically responded to Anna's unex-
pressed need and drew her down against him, holding
her in his arms. What had happened to his will-power,
his self-control, that same self-control that had enabled
him, with very little prior difficulty, to refuse to give in
to the temptation of satisfying his sexuality? He had lost
count of the number of times in the past he had turned
away from the opportunity to have a brief fling or even
begin a new relationship. The scars left by his marriage
had disillusioned him too much for him to want to risk
a second failure. His pride and his idealistic moral code
meant that he had never been tempted to indulge in sex
for its own sake...

And yet here he was, his body relaxed and at peace,
still washed by the soft echoes of the pleasure the
woman sleeping beside him had given him. And, even
worse, that pleasure had aroused the kind of emotional
response in him that he knew to be ironically farcical.

He actually felt protective of her, tender towards her; he actually *wanted* to hold her, to go on feeling the slender warmth of her body next to his own.

How could he, when he disliked and despised her, when everything he knew about her dictated that she was the last woman he could ever possibly love?

It was virtually impossible that her amnesia could have been faked, the nurse had told him, and she had obviously meant it, but *Ward* wasn't suffering from amnesia and he knew perfectly well that alongside the animosity that had crackled between them the first time they had met there had also been a very dangerous surge of mutual physical attraction. He also suspected that it was that which had led to Anna believing that they already shared a relationship, a past—and a bed...

However, that still did not explain how the woman he knew as a fraud and a cheat could suddenly be metamorphosed into someone so tender, so giving, so open and loving that she had literally taken his breath away.

No one had ever said the things to him that she had said, shown him so openly that he was desired and loved.

Loved!

His heartbeat stilled, and then started up again with heavy, potent, leaden strokes.

His body tensed.

What on earth was he going to do?

CHAPTER FIVE

'GOOD morning.'

Ward struggled to sit up, pushing his hand through his hair as the events of the previous night came flooding back.

'I've been awake for ages,' Anna told him, sitting up too, her face alight with love and happiness as she reached over to kiss him.

Ward groaned as the duvet slipped down, revealing the soft globes of her breasts. His fingers itched to pull it up again and cover her nakedness but Anna seemed to have no such inhibitions, pressing herself lovingly against him in a way that was so totally devoid of any manufactured kind of provocation or deliberate intent that Ward was helpless to prevent his body's response to her.

'You should have woken me,' Ward told her tersely, returning her kiss as perfunctorily as he could before saying, 'I'll go down and make us both some tea. How are you feeling, by the way?' he asked her. What was it the consultant had said he had to watch out for? Headaches, dizziness, blurred vision, nausea...

'Wonderful,' Anna told him softly, making no attempt to hide the smile curling her mouth. 'Totally, absolutely wonderful... Let's leave the tea for a while,' she added meaningfully, closing the distance he had put between them, her eyes suddenly shadowing a little as she confessed, 'All this between us feels so new to me, Ward. I...I still can't quite believe that it's really...that

I've been lucky enough to have met you. I know I must have told you all of this before, but after Ralph's death I felt so, so afraid that I...I didn't want to let anyone else into my life in case...in case...' She stopped and shook her head. 'The pain and shock of losing Ralph like that was...' She frowned. 'I felt so guilty as well. He was so young...alive one minute and then the next gone, and it seemed to me that it was safer not to let myself love anyone else ever again.

'He'd only taken the boat out on an impulse. Normally I'd have gone with him, even though I never really liked sailing that much. You can't grow up in Cornwall, though, and not know how to sail, or how important it is to respect the sea,' she added in a shaky voice. 'The coastguard said he must have been hit by a freak wave. He was an experienced sailor, cautious and not the sort of person who ever took any kind of risk.

'We were going to have dinner with his parents that night. I waited and waited and...'

She stopped, unable to go on, and Ward frowned. He had known from his enquiries that she had been widowed young and by a sailing accident, but he had assumed that her husband's death had been a result of some drunken revelry on the part of a group of young idiots. Now it seemed he had been wrong. The picture Anna had just painted for him was a very different one indeed, and there was no mistaking the emotion in her voice when she talked about her young husband.

'I don't know how I met you or why I changed my mind. I've always been so protective of my...my emotions...' She gave him a small smile. 'I can't pretend that I don't know exactly why, as a lover, you were able to turn over my decision to stay single...'

The dimples he had seen last night reappeared briefly

as she made this rueful disclosure. 'But what *does* puzzle me is how I ever came to let you get close enough to me for *that* to happen… I've never…How *did* we meet, Ward…?'

'The consultant said we were to let your memory return naturally,' Ward told her.

What she had just said to him had had a far more profound effect on him emotionally than he wanted to acknowledge—a very profound effect indeed.

'You must have loved him—Ralph—a lot,' he heard himself say gruffly. Well, better to keep her talking about her precious Ralph and the past than to run the risk of having her question *him* about *their* relationship again, and if he got out of bed as he had originally planned she would see, realise—

It shook him that he, a man who prided himself on his hard-headed pragmatism, should be so intensely and physically affected just because a woman smiled at him and said, 'Wonderful.'

'Well, yes, I did,' Anna agreed, but she was frowning slightly. 'It all seems so far away from me now and we were so very young. Our love for each other was… We grew up together and we'd always been a pair; people expected that we would marry. Our parents were friends and, whilst no one put any pressure on us to do so, and none of our parents would have wanted us to marry someone we *didn't* love, there was a sense of it being the right thing to do.

'Please don't misunderstand,' she begged him. 'We were very happy together, very content, but there was no… It wasn't like it is with you,' she told him huskily, lifting her glance to his as she added, 'But then I must have told you all of this before… What about you, though? Were you…have you been married?'

'Yes, briefly,' Ward told her tersely, 'but my marriage wasn't... It was a mistake for both of us.'

'Do you still love her?' Anna asked him hesitantly. Ward stared at her.

'Still *love* her?' He threw back his head and gave a bitter shout of laughter.

'No, I do not. For a long time after the divorce I think I probably hated her but, eventually, that died. If she was greedy and self-seeking, concerned only with her own wants and desires, then it was my fault for not realising it before we got married, and if she didn't like the fact that she was married to a workaholic who didn't have time to go out clubbing or throw his money around, then that was hers. The truth is that we both married a person who didn't exist. I accepted that she wasn't the woman I'd thought a long time ago.'

'You've forgiven her for her part in the break-up of your marriage,' Anna guessed wisely, 'but I don't think you've ever quite forgiven yourself.'

Ward was astounded. Her simple, direct statement was so true and yet no one else had ever recognised how he had felt, how much he blamed himself for making the wrong marriage.

'At least we didn't have any children.'

'You didn't want them?' Anna asked.

'*She* didn't want them,' he told her quietly.

'Ralph and I...We were so young and at first when he died I longed passionately to have a child, and sometimes even now...'

She gave a sad smile.

'Of course, I have my god-daughter, Beth. She lives here in Rye.' She paused. 'Oh, I'm sorry, you'll know all about her, of course.'

'Mmm...' Ward was deliberately non-committal but his brain was starting to work overtime.

If Anna had family here in town then surely it wouldn't be very long before they made contact with her. Then what was *he* going to do?

'I do hope that she and her friend Kelly will be able to continue making a success of their shop,' Anna continued chattily. 'Both of them have been spending quite a lot of time away on buying trips.

'I've helped out at the shop occasionally but I haven't been able to as often as I would have liked because of my other obligations.'

Her other obligations.

Ward's pulse quickened. Did she mean her partnership with Julian Cox? How could he question her further without arousing her suspicions?

'Mmm... I know you have a very busy life,' he agreed.

Anna frowned.

'Do I? I...' Her face suddenly crumpled. 'Oh, Ward, *I* don't know...I can't remember.'

He could hear the panic in her voice.

'When Mr Bannerman questioned me he said the last positive memory I had which he could date was some months ago. It was the weekend before Easter and it was my turn to do Meals on Wheels. Beth had invited me over for dinner...' She was beginning to look and sound increasingly distressed and Ward acted instinctively, reaching out towards her, intending only to calm and reassure her, but as she had done before Anna responded by wrapping her own arms around him.

Shivering a little, she begged, 'Oh, Ward, hold me, please... I feel so muddled... My head... My thoughts...'

'Then don't think,' Ward chided her.

'Don't *think*...' Anna had started to relax a little bit. She turned her head so that she could look into his eyes, and whispered against his mouth, 'Don't think...? Then what shall I do instead?'

It was a totally unnecessary question because she was already doing it—kissing him with such sweet fervour that Ward felt the back of his throat sting with raw emotion. No one had ever treated him like this, touched him like this, either physically or emotionally.

'Mmm...you taste nice,' Anna told him.

'So do you,' Ward responded gruffly. He could feel her nipples harden as they pressed against his chest. His own body was already aroused and eager.

Closing his eyes, he gave in to the swift tug of desire that ran through him like molten heat, dissolving the steel barrier of his self-control.

This time he knew exactly how to touch her and how to arouse her. She murmured blissfully when he kissed the side of her neck, her eyes tightly closed as she lay in his arms and encouraged him with soft, sensual little whispers of praise and love.

When it was her turn to touch him she was a little more hesitant, a little bit shy.

'I can't remember just what you like,' she told him uncertainly, her eyes grave and anxious.

'I like whatever you like, whatever you want to do,' Ward told her gently, and as he said the words he realised just how much he meant them.

'You might have to...to show me,' Anna warned him shyly, but they soon discovered he did not.

Anna seemed to know instinctively just where his body was most sensitive to her touch, and his throat arched tautly like a strong bow under the gentle assault of her open-mouthed kisses. His nipples turned into small, hard-tipped channels of pleasure that galvanised his whole body as she slowly kissed and then sucked on them. Now he knew just *why* she had trembled and arched so ecstatically against his hands when he had caressed her like that, but when she trailed her fingertips over the flat plane of his belly and bent her head to rim a fiery circle of pleasure around his navel Ward very quickly stopped her, his breath so tortured and hoarse that she looked anxiously at him.

'Come here,' he begged her rawly, exclaiming as he reached for her, 'You're a witch, do you know that? No one has ever made me feel like you do…made me want like you do…need like you do…' He groaned as he positioned her beneath him, shuddering wildly as he saw how eagerly and generously her body moved to accommodate him. There was such a generosity about her, such a sensuality, coupled with such a lack of wantonness that Ward was totally bemused by her.

'If I'm a witch, then you are definitely a magician,' Anna told him breathlessly several seconds later as her body quickened frantically to the fierce pace of his. The sex she and Ralph had shared had been pleasant, nice, but it had been nothing like this…nothing whatsoever. She had heard, of course, read, realised, but she had not known…never felt…

Oh, how could she have forgotten this? How could it have ever slipped from her memory? She was sure she would think of it and of Ward as the very last breath of life slipped from her body.

Anna had no idea she had said the words aloud at the summit of her climax until afterwards, until after she had felt the fierce, hot spurt of Ward's satisfaction spilling sensually into her body.

'You are the most…' Ward began as his lips gently grazed the length of her throat. He stopped and Anna looked at him, smiling through her emotional tears.

'I still can't quite believe we've got this, Ward,' she told him shakily. 'I still can't quite believe that it's real, that we've got each other. It just seems so wonderful, so magical…and I feel…' She touched her fingertips to his lips, her smile deepening as he couldn't resist catching hold of them and sucking slowly on them.

'I feel so blessed,' she finally told him sincerely. 'So very, very blessed.'

Blessed, but once she knew the truth she would feel *cursed*, Ward acknowledged.

She touched his jaw with her free hand.

'Mmm…you need a shave,' she commented.

Ward knew she was right; he could already see the slight rash his overnight stubble had caused on the fair skin of her breast.

'Er…yes…' Suddenly he was totally alert. 'I…I left my stuff in my car. I'll have to go and get it and whilst I'm up I may as well go and get a paper as well.'

'Oh, but I thought you said you'd brought your things in last night,' Anna objected.

'Er…yes, I did…but not my razor…'

'Oh, well, if you are going out for a paper, why don't I come with you and—?'

'No! No…' That was the last thing Ward wanted. Getting a paper had simply been an excuse to allow him to drive over to the hotel, pay his bill and collect his things.

'No. The consultant said you had to rest,' he reminded Anna more gently. 'I'll get the paper and then we'll have something to eat and…'

'What day is it?' Anna asked him, suddenly anxious.

'Sunday,' Ward told her promptly, glad to have her ask a question he could answer honestly.

'Oh, so you don't need to be at work. What is your job, Ward?'

'I don't have one,' he told her. 'At least, I sold out my business interests some time ago, and now I've got some consultancy work to do from time to time and my investments...'

'Investments.' Anna started to frown, her forehead crinkling. 'Oh, that rings a bell. I...'

Whilst Ward held his breath she shook her head regretfully.

'No, it's gone...gone... Is *that* how we met?' she asked him curiously. 'Did you come to advise me on my investments?'

Ward just about managed to conceal his reaction. He advised *her* on investments!

'I'm not telling you anything,' he responded. 'Remember...'

'I know... The consultant said it would all come back naturally,' Anna agreed with a sigh. 'You go and get your paper, then. Oh, and would you bring one for me?'

Bring one for her? Which one? Naturally he was supposed to know which paper she would read.

Whoever had made that comment about deceit and tangled webs had certainly known exactly what they were talking about, Ward decided grimly as he got out of bed.

CHAPTER SIX

TUCKING the newspapers he had just bought under his arm, Ward quickened his step as he hurried back to his car. It had taken him rather longer than he had planned to check out of the hotel and make his way back to Anna's home. He only hoped that the paper he had bought for her would be to her taste. It had seemed a fairly safe bet; his mother read it.

He had almost reached his car when his attention was caught by the display of fresh flowers at a small outdoor stall.

Ward hesitated, looked at the blooms, turned away and made to walk past, but then changed his mind and turned to walk in the direction of the stall.

The friendly young woman who had served him was certainly a persuasive salesperson, he acknowledged ruefully ten minutes later as he opened the boot of his car to place the newspapers and the bouquet of flowers he had just bought in it.

He had no idea what Anna's taste in flowers was but there was no denying that the artistically arranged assortment of soft cream blooms spiked with dark green foliage and varying shades of lilac to deepest purple, both looked and smelled attractive.

It was only when he was in the car and on his way back to Anna's home that he thought to question just what he was doing buying a bouquet of flowers for a woman whom he claimed to dislike and despise.

He had bought them because it was the sort of gesture

she would probably expect, he told himself defensively. That was all. There was no more personal meaning behind the gesture. After all, it wasn't as though he had bought her red roses, was it? His actions certainly hadn't been inspired by any kind of tender feelings for her. That was impossible. Wasn't it? The very thought that he might be guilty of such uncharacteristic behaviour made Ward scowl darkly.

He was still scowling five minutes later when, having retrieved everything from the boot of his car, he walked up to Anna's front door and rang the bell.

Anna had used Ward's absence to good effect; she had had a shower, dressed in a pair of soft chambray trousers and a comfortable white shirt and then she had gone downstairs and started to prepare their breakfast.

When she opened the front door to him, the first thing that Ward could smell was the appetisingly rich aroma of freshly ground coffee; the second, as she leaned forward to take the flowers he was handing her, was Anna's perfume.

It must be because he was hungry that he had experienced that peculiar heart-stopping moment of dizziness, Ward decided as he closed the front door behind himself.

'Flowers. Oh, Ward, they're so beautiful,' Anna breathed ecstatically. 'And you chose my favourites... Oh, Ward...' Her eyes were bright with happy tears as Anna looked up at him. 'I was just thinking again when you were gone how very, very lucky I am.'

Ward closed his eyes and turned away from her so that she wouldn't see his expression. By rights he ought to feel pleased that she was exposing her emotions to him like this; that she was putting herself in his power, in a position where, ultimately, he would have the ability to humiliate her. But for some reason what he did feel was a confusing mixture of anger and pain—anger because she was so recklessly and foolishly leaving herself unprotected and at his mercy, and pain...

Ward had no idea why he should feel pain and, what was more, he didn't want to know.

'You could have used your key, you know,' Anna was telling him conversationally as she led the way back to the kitchen.

His key!

Ward opened his mouth to tell her that he didn't possess a key to her house and then closed it again.

'You've got time to go up and have a shave before breakfast,' Anna told him, pausing before saying ruefully, 'I didn't know...what you'd like, but I have to confess there isn't much choice. I must have planned to go shopping yesterday, I think.'

Anna had been dismayed to discover how little there was in her fridge to satisfy the appetite of a man the size of Ward. Somehow, even without the benefit of her memory, she doubted that he would be happy to eat the simple breakfast of bio yoghurt and raw fruit which she knew instinctively she preferred. There was wholemeal bread and eggs and, to her relief, she had found some smoked salmon in her freezer along with a leg of lamb. They could have the lamb for lunch and then tomorrow she would shop for proper man-filling food. Odd. What an odd thing memory was; she knew, for instance, exactly where the shops were and how to cook, but she had no idea of Ward's culinary tastes.

'I'll have whatever's going,' Ward told her almost brusquely. At home he lived and ate simply. He could cook, when he had to, but eating solitary meals did not encourage him to spend time in the kitchen preparing

them so he normally relied on ready-prepared supermarket ones or ate out.

Whilst he was upstairs, Anna arranged her flowers,
humming happily to herself. They really were beautiful,
her favourite colours, and she quickly coaxed them into
a lovely soft, relaxed display.

Upstairs in the bedroom they had shared the previous
night, Ward deliberately ignored the now neatly remade
bed. He still couldn't understand how he had come to
behave in the way he had.

To simply say that the opportunity she had presented
had been too much of a temptation for him to resist was
too simplistic and just didn't lie easily on his con-
science. He had always been so controlled, so in control
of himself and his desires. From both his mother and
his stepfather he had learned the value of respecting
both himself and others. Casual sex, once he had been
past the experimental eagerness of his extreme youth,
had simply never been something which held any ap-
peal for him.

He swallowed hard as he made his way to the bathroom with his razor. Even now, just thinking about last
night made him feel…made him want… Ward clenched
his jaw. Well, what he wanted he certainly could not
have, he informed himself sternly. Last night had been
a mistake which wasn't going to be repeated tonight.

But Anna thought that they were lovers and she
would expect them to share a bed, he reminded himself.

Maybe, but that didn't mean that he had to *touch* her,
did it? It didn't mean that he had to stroke her silky
skin or kiss her soft mouth; it didn't mean he had to…

Hell!

Why on earth had he started to think about that—
about her? It had been an accident, an error of judge-

ment, something that should never have happened and most certainly would never ever happen again.

'I hope you like smoked salmon and scrambled eggs,' Anna told Ward ruefully as he came into the kitchen. He looked so handsome, all freshly shaved and smelling subtly of something tangy and slightly citrusy. She was glad he wasn't the kind of man to wear a heavy, ostentatious aftershave, but even though he looked and smelled good now there had been something very special and erotic, something deeply personal and intimate about the way he had smelled—and tasted—last night.

Anna blushed a little as she realised where her thoughts were taking her—and why.

Heavens, if Ward were to suggest that they forget about breakfast and feast off one another instead, she knew she would be very easily persuaded to agree. The way she had behaved last night was totally outside her own experience of herself, and she had to confess that once she had got over the shock of her physical desire for Ward she had positively enjoyed the liberating experience of exploring her own sensuality.

Smoked salmon and scrambled eggs. Ward's eyes lit up and his mouth started to water; it was one of his favourite breakfast dishes.

'Wonderful,' he told Anna warmly, unable to take his eyes off her face as he saw the pretty way she started to blush. Surely this wasn't how a woman of her type should behave, blushing just because he had shown approval of her choice of breakfast?

Anna could have told him that it wasn't so much that that was making her skin colour up so rosily as the fact that she felt so euphorically happy, so sensually sensitive and aware that she was very tempted to ignore the habit of a lifetime and take the initiative by suggesting boldly to him that they take their breakfast back to bed.

Instead, she told him a little breathlessly, 'I...er...found a bottle of champagne. It's in the fridge. If you could open it we could have Buck's Fizz...'

Champagne!

Ward's eyebrows rose.

'It...I...'

What was his voice implying? Anna wondered. That she was being extravagant, both emotionally and financially, going over the top, perhaps? It was so frustrating not being able to rely on her knowledge of him, her previous experience with him, to judge what his reactions meant or what his views were.

'It doesn't matter if you'd rather not,' she began hesitantly, and then changed her mind. Honesty was a vital component of any relationship so far as she was concerned, even if sometimes it had to be softened a little with tact.

Her head held high, she told Ward, 'I wanted to make this special. Memorable.' Her face flushed rosily again as she added truthfully, '*You* made last night so very special for me. I may not be able to recall the memories, the special times we've already had together, Ward, but at least I can make sure that the new ones we're creating now are good ones. For me, this morning will be a first celebration of our love for one another and our relationship. Although perhaps the champagne *is* a little excessive...'

She paused and gave him a wry smile. 'If you'd rather not...'

For a moment Ward was too caught off guard to speak. The words she had used, the emotions she had just expressed, had made him shockingly, shamingly aware of just what he had done.

But *she* wasn't really the person she now appeared to be, he reassured himself fiercely. In reality the words she was saying to him meant nothing; the emotions she had expressed just did not exist, *could* not exist in the woman he knew her to be. But how could she possibly manufacture such a very different personality from her own? Ward had to admit that he didn't know and that perhaps he should have questioned the hospital consultant a little more thoroughly.

By rights he knew full well that the last thing he should be doing was toasting a relationship, a *love* that simply did not exist with Buck's Fizz, whilst eating *à deux* with a woman who was completely unaware of the real situation between them, but as he looked into Anna's eager, happy face Ward knew that there was no way he could disappoint her.

They ate their breakfast in Anna's sunny conservatory, with Missie curled up in her basket and the cat, Whittaker, basking in a pool of sunlight.

'I'll help you clear up,' Ward offered when they had finished. Smiling at him, Anna got up. She had put his flowers on a small side table and as she caught sight of them her smile deepened. Instead of starting to clear the table she walked to Ward's side and leaned over him, one hand on his shoulder, the other very gently, hesitantly almost, touching his face as she bent her head to kiss him.

'Thank you again for my beautiful flowers,' she told him softly.

It wasn't a passionate or intimate kiss, just the soft brush of her mouth against his—nothing really, Ward would tell himself angrily later, and certainly no reason for him to reach out and slide his arms around her body, pulling her onto his knee, his mouth fastening hungrily over hers, one arm cradling her against his body whilst he lifted his free hand to slide it behind her head so that he could hold the nape of her neck as his mouth fed greedily on hers.

Anna almost felt as though she would swoon with delight.

When she had made that abrupt decision to kiss Ward she had hoped, of course, that he would respond, reciprocate, but the intensity of his response had exceeded even the most adventurous of her hopes. She forgot that she was thirty-seven years old, that she was a woman whose desires were far more cerebral than physical. Her mouth opened beneath Ward's, her tongue twining sensuously with his. Beneath the hand she had originally placed against his chest to steady herself she could feel the suddenly accelerated thud of his heartbeat. The still warm air of the conservatory was filled with the sound of their breathing and the soft, frantic endearments Anna was whispering to Ward against his mouth.

Already her body was starting to ache with need for him, all the wild, sweet, wanton feelings she had experienced with him before rushing back over her.

The soft weight of her body pressing against him combined with the responsive murmur of her voice as she responded to his kiss was too much for Ward's precarious self-control. His mind might deplore what he was doing, but his body was working on a very different agenda.

His hand shook as he unfastened the buttons of Anna's shirt and then slipped it off her shoulder so that he could kiss the fragrant warmth of her skin. A tiny rash of goose bumps betrayed her responsive reaction to him and through the sheer transparency of her ivory-coloured bra he could see the dark burgeoning of her nipples.

Now it was his turn to vocalise his desire, and Anna shivered deliciously beneath the warm gust of his breath against her breast as he whispered her name.

As Ward bent his head down towards her, a shaft of sunlight touched the exposed nape of his neck, burnishing his thick dark hair, highlighting not just his masculinity but also an unbearably poignant vulnerability which touched Anna's emotions so intensely that her eyes filled with tears.

Very gently she stroked his exposed nape, almost as a mother might a child. Mother and child—immediately the images her thoughts conjured up sent a shocking surge of emotion right through her body. What had Ward been like as a child? What would it be like to have his child?

Ward's mouth nudged aside the fabric of her bra, his tonguetip circling urgently around her nipple. Anna shuddered wildly as her body reacted compulsively to his touch, all thoughts of anything other than what was happening between them forgotten. Ward's mouth covered her nipple, hot, wet, tugging urgently on her eager flesh.

Anna's dining chairs, charming though they were, had not been designed for the use they were currently putting them to and, although she had impatiently tugged Ward's shirt free of his trousers, right now Anna needed far more intimate contact with his body than their present situation allowed.

'Ward... Ward...' she whispered frantically in his ear. 'Let's go upstairs...to bed...'

The sound of her voice brought Ward back to reality.
What on earth was he *doing*? Yes, what was *she* doing?
his body protested as he slowly released Anna's nipple
and slid the silky fabric of her bra back over her damp
breast.

As Anna slid shakily off his lap Ward knew he had
to do something—say something—and quickly, because
if—*once* they were upstairs... His body was already
very powerfully making its protest felt. It wanted Anna
right back where she had been, or, even better, where
she had been last night—in his bed, in his arms, her
body clothed only in the heat generated by their mutual
desire. But Ward couldn't afford to give in to the dic-
tates of his body, no matter how urgently it was ex-
pressing them.

Instead, he caught hold of Anna's hand whilst determinedly keeping some distance between them.

'Anna...' When she looked at him like that he lost
all sense of what he wanted to say; all he could do was
shake his head and tell her bluntly and hoarsely, 'I
can't...'

He *couldn't*! Anna's eyes widened. What on earth...?
And then she flushed as she realised what he must
mean. They weren't a young couple at the height of
their sexual powers, after all, and last night and then
this morning they had—

It was different for a woman. She didn't need...she
could... But then Ward had...

As he saw the uncertain, discreet little look she gave
his body Ward suddenly realised what Anna was thinking.

A little wryly he wondered how she would react if
he were to tell her that not only was he perfectly capable
of making love with her but that if he took her to bed

now he doubted that *once* was going to satisfy the fierce, pulsing ache which was tormenting a body almost incandescent with desire for her. The barrier which was preventing him from making love with her wasn't a physical but a moral one. But he could hardly tell her that! And perhaps it might be a good idea to make sure that he was not confronted with any more temptation.

To that end, as soon as they had finished clearing away after their meal Ward said to Anna, 'It's a nice day; I was wondering if you would like to go out somewhere, perhaps for a drive or a walk...'

'Well, we could possibly do both,' Anna answered. 'We could call at the garden centre; I noticed when you were out this morning that I must have been working on planting up some containers when I had my accident and I obviously need some more plants to finish them off. There's a good garden centre on the other side of town, and since it's not far from the river we could park the car and walk along the river path, if that appeals to you.'

At the sound of the word 'walk' Missie, who had been lying in her basket, jumped up and started to bark excitedly.

'Looks like the decision's already been made for us,' Ward told Anna ruefully.

'What are your hobbies?' Anna asked him hesitantly half an hour later when she was seated beside him in his car as he drove in the direction she had described to him.

'Work, work and more work,' Ward told her dryly and honestly. 'I like walking,' he added equally truthfully, 'but I'm afraid I seldom make time to do any even though my farmhouse is right up in the hills.'

'You're a workaholic, but you said you were retired,' Anna pointed out, confused.

'Yes, I am, sort of... I sold up my company but I'm still involved in consultancy work.'

'You mentioned investments before,' Anna remembered, her forehead crinkling as she gave a small shiver. For some reason the word 'investments' made her feel anxious and tense, as though a large shadow had been cast over the warmth of the sun shining so brightly outside the car.

Ward gave her a quick look. Was she going to start remembering, and what was she going to do if she did— no, *when* she did? he corrected himself sternly. When she did he would be only too relieved, because then he could insist on her repaying Ritchie's money and then once that was done he could walk away from her and get on with his own life.

'Is that how we met? Were you...did you advise me on my investments?' Anna asked him uncertainly, repeating her earlier question to him. She didn't understand why the subject should make her feel so unhappy and ill at ease.

'Hardly,' Ward told her curtly, unable to stop himself from adding, 'Investment advice is the *last* thing *you'd* need or want from anyone.'

Confused, Anna was just about to ask him to explain his cryptic remark when she realised they were coming to a roundabout and that she'd have to give him directions. By the time they were on the right road, a small inner voice of caution had warned her that some things, like Pandora's box, were best left unmeddled with. Maybe she and Ward had quarrelled over the subject; maybe he had offered her advice and help and she had been too independent to take it. Whatever the case, she would be much better able to deal with it once her memory had returned, she told herself firmly.

Ward wondered suspiciously why Anna was not pursuing the subject and demanding to know more. *Had* she remembered? Instinctively he knew that she couldn't have done, but who knew how far back in her past her double dealings went? Who knew how long she had been cheating and deceiving others?

'Here we are; it's this lane on the left,' Anna told him, directing his attention to the entrance to the garden centre.

At Anna's suggestion Ward remained in the car with Missie whilst she went to get her plants. Although she would not have dreamed of saying so to him, Ward's cryptic remark to her had left her feeling hurt and confused, her manner towards him noticeably cooler than it had been, Ward was aware as she gently refused his company. This was a woman who would never descend to angry arguments or sullen silence but who could, nevertheless, very firmly retreat into her own space when she felt the need, Ward recognised, unwillingly admiring her distancing air of dignity as she quietly closed the car door and walked away from him.

Everything about her spoke of gentleness and dignity, of a woman who put the needs of others above her own, a woman whose behaviour was governed by a slightly old-fashioned moral code, a code which he acknowledged was very similar to his own. And yet she had still joined forces with Julian Cox in his despicably fraudulent activities. On her way towards the store, Ward was not surprised to see her stop to aid an elderly couple who were having trouble lifting an unwieldy pot plant into the boot of their car.

CHAPTER SEVEN

WARD glanced frowningly at his watch.

Anna had been gone for over half an hour, having told him she would be about ten minutes.

He looked at Missie. She was fast asleep, curled up on the blanket on the back seat of his car. Checking that a window was open enough to let in fresh air for her, he climbed out of the car and locked it, setting out in the direction Anna had taken.

He found her less than five minutes later, standing next to a car filled with plants. She had her back to him and her face was turned up towards that of the man standing next to her, who, if his besotted expression was anything to go by, was thoroughly enjoying the experience. As Anna's soft laughter rang out, Ward was suddenly stabbed by a surge of dislike for her male companion that was so strong, it literally momentarily deprived him of breath.

Angrily he told himself that the feeling pounding through him was caused merely by his apprehension that Anna's companion might inadvertently have said something to her to make her suspicious of his own supposed relationship with her, thereby foiling his plans to punish her, and that it had nothing to do with something more personal—something, in fact, which was far, far more dangerous.

Anxiously he hurried towards Anna but, as Ward approached her, the man with her reached out and touched her arm, drawing her closer to him in order to allow someone to pass her. As he saw the man put his hand on Anna's arm, a murderous flash of emotion sliced through Ward. Without knowing how he had got there he suddenly discovered he was standing at Anna's side, his gaze challenging the other man's right to touch her.

'Oh, Ward!' Anna exclaimed. His appearance at her side had both startled her and somehow made her feel a little guilty. 'I'm sorry I was so long,' she said, mistaking the cause of his black-browed look. 'There was a long queue at the till and then I was just on my way back when I bumped into Tim.'

As Anna started to introduce them Ward forced himself to respond to the other man's uncertain smile.

He knew from the look in Anna's eyes that she had no suspicion whatsoever that he wasn't who she thought him to be, but for some reason his angry anxiety refused to subside, and so did his dislike of the man at her side. What was the matter with him? he asked himself irritably. Anyone would think he was jealous. *Jealous*. The very idea was ridiculous...laughable, impossible. He never got jealous. In fact he didn't have a jealous bone in his body.

'I'm sorry you had to wait so long.' Anna apologised again quietly once they were on their own.

She was silent after that as they walked back to the car but Ward was well aware that she kept watching him, looking at him.

'I only came to look for you because Missie was getting fretful,' Ward told Anna untruthfully as they approached the car. Anna said nothing but Ward could see the quick look she gave the peacefully sleeping dog as he placed her plants into the car boot.

Ten minutes later, as they headed silently for the river path, Missie tugging a little impatiently on her lead,

Ward acknowledged that he had perhaps overreacted. Had the situation been different, had they been a real couple, he might have been able to lower his pride enough to admit his jealousy, but how could he admit to feeling jealous about a woman he didn't even like, never mind love?

It was just his natural male instincts coming to the fore, he tried to tell himself as he helped Anna over the stile that led to the footpath.

As they walked side by side along the river, Anna acknowledged how daunting she was beginning to find the fact that she knew so little about Ward. His anger had confused and upset her. It had seemed completely at odds with the way he had behaved towards her previously. Was he, perhaps, a very impatient man?

She watched as he paused whilst a young woman with three young children and two dogs went through the turnstile ahead of them. One of the dogs and the youngest child had to be coaxed through. Ward waited patiently, even offering to hold one of the dogs' leads for the harassed young mother, who flashed him a grateful smile. Not the action of an impatient man, Anna admitted as she instinctively moved closer to him, her hand touching his arm in a gesture of female possession. The young woman meant no harm, but even so…Anna was both surprised and a little bewildered by the strength of her own feelings.

Her eyes flashed a little as she saw the way Ward was smiling at the young mother. How dared he look at her like that, smile at her like that…*flirt* with her like that?

Her head had begun to ache and she felt tired.

'I think I'd like to go back to the car,' she told Ward woodenly. Without waiting for his response she turned round and started to walk quickly in the direction she had just come, both ashamed of and overwhelmed by her own emotions.

As he drove them back to Anna's house, Ward reflected inwardly that Anna had every right to be annoyed with him. He *had* overreacted in the garden centre, but admitting his fault and his jealousy would mean admitting emotions he couldn't possibly allow himself to feel. He was losing track of the real reason for his presence in Anna's life, her home...her bed... His body was confusing and betraying him with its passionate response to her.

By the time they reached her house Anna's head was pounding nauseously, but a headache was no excuse for her behaviour. How *could* she have been so jealous of that poor, harassed young mother? She could sense that ordinarily such emotions were totally foreign to her and yet she *had* experienced them and that confused her. Even frightened her, she admitted to herself.

The telephone was ringing as they walked into the house. Anna went to answer it, one hand massaging her aching temple as she recognised her god-daughter's voice.

'Beth! How are you?'

'Fine...and you?'

Anna hesitated for a moment. She just didn't feel up to coping with Beth's concern and questions if she told her the truth.

'I'm fine,' she fibbed.

'I meant to ring earlier,' Beth told her, 'but I didn't get back until this morning. The family all send their love, by the way. Mum said to remind you that it's their silver wedding soon; she's planning a big party and, of course, she wants you there.'

Anna released her breath slowly. Beth must have been home to visit her parents in Cornwall. No doubt she, Anna, *had* known about her trip even though she couldn't remember .

'Look, I must go. We'll talk again soon,' Beth was saying, and before Anna could reply the younger woman was saying goodbye and ending the call.

In the living room of the accommodation above the shop, Beth closed her eyes and gave a small sigh.

She knew she had been a little abrupt with Anna, but her godmother was always so intuitive and aware that Beth was afraid she might guess... Quickly she scanned through the post she had picked up on her way in, her body tensing as she saw the airmail envelope from Prague.

Her mouth went dry as she ripped it open. Inside was a copy despatch note for some of the pottery she had bought for the shop during her buying trip to Prague earlier in the year. She was still waiting for the gorgeous reproduction antique crystal. Only the previous week her partner, Kelly, had mentioned that it was disappointing that it had still not arrived.

'When exactly is it coming? What exactly did happen about that?' she had asked curiously.

'Soon,' Beth had told her quickly, crossing her fingers behind her back. 'Very soon.'

She had been conscious of the searching look Kelly had given her. They had known one another since university and she was just grateful that Kelly's newly engaged status meant that she was too involved with her new fiancé to probe too deeply into the delayed arrival of the Czech crystal. It had been bad enough having her stupidity over Julian Cox made public without...

Angrily Beth closed her eyes. Her emotions were still too raw and sensitive. It was just as well that Kelly was out of town with Brough, visiting his family. Her godmother's voice had sounded a little strained on the telephone. If she had hurt her feelings by being distant with her recently, she would have to find a way of making it up to her...later...when she felt more able to. For now she intended to avoid her godmother as much as she could. The last thing she wanted was for Anna to guess...To guess what? That she had made a fool of herself over a man a second time?

'What is it? What's wrong?' Ward asked Anna sharply as he saw the way she was massaging and rubbing her temple. She looked very pale, very heavy-eyed.

'I've got a headache,' Anna told him warily.

'A headache!' Immediately Ward was at her side. 'Since when? Why didn't you say something? Do you feel sick? Can you—'

'Ward, it's a headache, that's all,' Anna snapped, immediately regretting her small loss of patience when she saw his expression.

Mindful of what the consultant had said to him, Ward watched her grimly. The last thing he wanted to do was panic her, but...

'Come on,' he told her quietly, taking hold of her arm.

'Where are we going?' Anna protested. 'I was just going to put the lunch on...'

'Hospital,' Ward told her, ignoring the second half of her statement.

'Hospital? Why? I...'

'The consultant warned me to be alert for any symptoms such as a headache, nausea, or blurred vision,' he told her gently.

'It's just a headache…that's all… I haven't got blurred vision.' Anna started to panic but she still allowed Ward to guide her out to the car.

Luckily the hospital's casualty department was relatively quiet, and even more fortunately the consultant who had seen her last night was actually on duty. At Anna's insistence Ward remained with her whilst the consultant questioned her and then examined her.

'Hmm…' he announced when he had finished. 'Are you normally prone to headaches?' he asked Anna.

'Sometimes… I do get the odd tension headache,' she admitted.

'I tend to think that this is what this one is,' he diagnosed. 'So far as I can judge there certainly isn't anything to indicate that it might be anything else. You say that so far you haven't remembered anything of the time that you've lost…no flashbacks…?'

'No, nothing,' Anna told him dispiritedly.

'You see, I *told* you it was just a headache,' she said tiredly once they were back in the car.

'I know, but it still had to be checked out,' Ward responded.

She had looked so forlorn, so…so sad, sitting there whilst the consultant asked her if she could remember anything yet, that Ward had ached to take hold of her, to wrap his arms protectively around her and tell her that everything was all right, that she was safe; that it didn't matter a damn to him if she never remembered… That he would—

Anna gave a startled gasp as he changed gear almost viciously, throwing her against her seat belt.

'Sorry,' he muttered, avoiding meeting her gaze as he swung the car into her drive.

Once they were back in the house Ward went straight upstairs. He had seen some headache tablets in the cabinet in the bathroom. Removing two, he went back downstairs and filled a glass with water.

Anna had her back to him as she placed the lamb in the roasting tin. Going up to her, he tapped her on the shoulder and handed her the glass and the tablets, saying quietly, 'Take these. They might help.'

Tears blurred Anna's eyes. She was so unused to having anyone look after her, take care of her...love her. To her own consternation as much as Ward's, her whole body started to shake as her emotions overwhelmed her.

Pushing past Ward, she dashed upstairs. This was ridiculous. She was behaving idiotically.

Ward caught up with her just as she pushed open her bedroom door.

'Anna, what is it? What have I done?' he demanded worriedly.

What had *he* done. Anna shook her head.

'It isn't you, it's me,' she told him through her tears. 'This morning, on the footpath...that young mother... I was so jealous, but I don't get jealous, and you were just helping her, but I thought...I felt... For a moment I wanted...' Anna stopped, too ashamed of herself to go on.

'I hated her, Ward,' she finally admitted huskily. 'I hated the way she smiled at you and...and the way you looked back at her...I wanted...'

Ward stared at her.

'Was *that* what caused your headache?' he demanded.

Anna gave a small smile.

'No, the headache was already there, but it did cause me some *heartache*,' she admitted ruefully. 'Ward, I was so jealous...'

Ward took a deep breath. Her honesty and her bravery compelled him to be equally open with her.

'I was jealous too...earlier...in the garden centre. That man...Tim...he was touching your arm and I wanted to...I could have...'

'You were jealous of Tim and not angry because I had been so long? Oh, Ward, Tim is just a friend and he's very happily married...' Laughter gurgled in Anna's throat. 'You couldn't possibly have been jealous of him...'

'And you couldn't possibly have been jealous of that poor young woman.'

Somehow or other Ward discovered he had taken Anna in his arms and now she was nestling happily against his body, lifting her tear-stained face to his.

'I suppose the trouble is that our love is still so new that we aren't quite sure of one another yet. Our feelings are still very...very intense...very...passionate...' Anna concluded, her voice dropping to a whisper and her glance following the gentle touch of Ward's fingertip as he started to trace the shape of her jaw and then her mouth.

Anna's lips parted on a small, beatific sigh. Ward's fingertip met the soft breath she expelled. It sent a shaft of fierce pleasure right through his body. Anna moved her head a little, capturing his fingertip in her mouth. Very, very slowly she started to suck on it.

Ward felt as though his insides had been turned to pure molten pleasure. Honesty was a very dangerous aphrodisiac, he decided dizzily as Anna gave a little

moan of pleasure before starting to nibble on a second
finger.

'Have you any idea just what that is doing to me?'
Ward grumbled despairingly.

'Mmm…No… Why don't you tell me?' Anna invited
seductively.

'Well, it might feel a little bit like this,' Ward
obliged, instigating a little bit of seduction of his own
by nibbling gently on her neck.

'Mmm…' Anna sighed appreciatively, closing her
eyes.

'You know, you really do wear too many clothes,'
Ward whispered thickly to her several seconds later as
he helped to correct this sartorial error by removing her
shirt.

'Mmm… I could say the same about you,' Anna
agreed huskily. If Ward responded so satisfactorily to
just the delicate touch of her mouth against his fingers,
then how would he react if she repeated that caress on
other more sensitive parts of his body? Anna wondered
daringly.

She and Ralph had never really experimented with
sex. They had both been a little shy and almost formal
with one another in their lovemaking, but now Anna
was beginning to discover a spirit of sensual adventure
within herself that both bemused and excited her. Her
fingers tugged impatiently at Ward's buttons whilst she
nuzzled the warm flesh of his throat. His skin smelled
just as it had done last night—slightly musky, warm and
very, very male.

'Mmm…you taste good,' Ward told her, echoing her
own thoughts about him as his lips started to caress the
soft curve of her breast.

Anna had no idea just how long it took them to remove each other's clothes; she only knew that once they had she couldn't stop herself from openly feasting her gaze and then her hands and mouth on Ward's body.

Initially he was tempted to stop her. He wasn't used to a passive role, but Anna was gently insistent.

'I've never been like this before,' she told him quietly.

'How do you know,' Ward questioned her, 'if you can't remember?'

'I just *know*,' Anna told him simply, and against all logic, as he looked into her eyes, Ward believed her.

There was nothing practised or artificial about her touch, and Ward controlled his own desire to watch her tenderly as she explored his body with absorbed concentration.

'Everything, *all* of you, is just so perfect,' she whispered, pink-cheeked, at one point, giving him an indignant look when Ward started to laugh.

'Twenty years ago I might, *just might*, have been tempted to believe you,' he said. 'But now...' His laugh, warm and uninhibited, shook his body.

'It's true, though,' Anna protested, injured. 'You are perfect—to me...'

'Aha...' Ward began, but Anna stopped him.

She demanded huskily, 'Ward, were you really jealous of Tim?'

'Really,' he confirmed steadily, holding her gaze before adding truthfully, 'Very!'

Anna gave a small loving sigh.

'You don't have any need to be, you know,' she told him frankly. 'I never thought I'd ever feel like this.' She paused. 'Did you...*have* there been...?'

'No...not now,' Ward replied promptly. 'My mother...' He stopped abruptly.

'Tell me about your family, Ward,' Anna encouraged, her fingers playing with the soft, dark hair that covered his chest.

'No, there isn't very much to tell, and no, you haven't met them,' Ward answered. This was a subject he didn't want to pursue but Anna obviously wasn't going to be sidetracked.

'Tell me about your home,' she insisted. 'Have I seen it?'

'No!'

Ward reached up and drew her down against his body, cupping her face as he started to kiss her. It might be a good way of silencing her, he acknowledged several seconds later, but it still possessed dangers of its own. He had already told himself that, no matter what the temptation, he was not going to succumb to it or make the same mistakes he had made last night, but Anna's fingertips were gently stroking down the length of his body and just the thought of how it would feel to have them caressing the most intimate part of him was enough to make him give a small gasp of awed awareness.

'You're so big,' she told him, wide-eyed, as she touched him.

Ward looked at her a little suspiciously but there was no trace of any guile in her expression. In fact, if he were a vain man, he could, he acknowledged, be very, very susceptible to the look in Anna's eyes, urgent now as she studied his body.

'And you're so...you're so you,' he told her thickly as he reached out for her.

After that it was a long time before either of them said anything remotely intelligible, although neither of them seemed to have any difficulty in interpreting the other's whispered words of pleasure and incandescent delight.

'Oh, Ward,' Anna whispered, torn between emotional tears of release and happy laughter as she lay trembling in Ward's arms in the aftermath of their lovemaking.

'Oh, Ward, what?' he demanded wryly.

'Oh, Ward, I'm just so glàd that you're a part of my life, that I met you, that you're here with me… like…like this…' Anna told him softly.

Ward paused for a moment.

'No more than I am,' he told her gruffly.

For a moment Ward could hardly believe what he had said. His admission had been tantamount to a declaration of love. What the hell was he doing… thinking…feeling…?

'Ward?'

He tensed as Anna suddenly shot up in bed, her voice anxious. What had happened? Had she suddenly recovered her memory? Was she…?

'What is it? What's wrong?' he asked her tersely.

'I never fed poor Missie and Whittaker. Oh, and the lamb's still waiting to be cooked…'

'Stay here,' Ward told her masterfully. 'I'll go down and sort everything out.' He was only gone a couple of minutes, and when he came back he was smiling broadly.

'What is it?' Anna demanded suspiciously as he climbed back into bed beside her. 'Why are you smiling like that?'

'I think you can forget about the lamb,' he told her jovially. 'Oh, and Missie and Whittaker *don't* need feeding either.'

Anna guessed immediately what had happened.

'Oh, no. They've eaten the lamb,' she wailed.

'Oh, yes, I'm afraid they have,' Ward chuckled. 'They must have got tired of waiting for us and decided to help themselves.'

'Oh, but Ward, there isn't anything for *us* to eat,' Anna complained.

'Who needs food?' Ward responded recklessly.

'Mmm…Who needs anything else when we've got what we've got?' Anna agreed dreamily.

CHAPTER EIGHT

'AND so as I was saying, Anna, if you could swop with me and do my next week's Meals on Wheels rota, I would—'

Anna's visitor broke off, her eyes rounding in surprise, her face going pink as Ward came strolling into the kitchen.

'I've changed the tyre on your car. Just as well I noticed that you'd got a slow puncture,' Ward told Anna.

'Er...Mary, this is Ward, my...my friend...' Anna said hastily, correctly interpreting the curiosity in the other woman's face.

'Oh, yes...I see... Your...friend...I didn't know. I...er... Look, I really must be going. Nice to have met you...er...Ward...'

'What was all that about?' Ward asked Anna after Mary had gone.

'She wanted me to change rotas with her for her Meals on Wheels,' Anna told him.

Ward started to frown.

It was three days now since he had moved in with Anna and so far she had shown no signs of her memory returning—and so far, too, he had shown no signs of keeping his promise to himself and putting a safe distance between them.

In fact...

He grimaced to himself, remembering the way Anna

had coaxed him last night, whispering to him, 'It's silly you sleeping in this bed and me having to...'

'The consultant said you needed to *rest*,' Ward had reminded her stoically.

'Mmm...but how will you know if I get a bad headache or something in the night if we aren't sleeping together?' Anna had asked him teasingly.

There had been no contest, of course, and this morning he had woken up with Anna tucked neatly into the curve of his body, and then... But that wasn't the complication which was making him frown now. Sooner or later someone was going to question his appearance in Anna's life and he couldn't afford to have that happen, not at this stage. When Anna got her memory back then he would be able to deal with whatever accusations she chose to make against him. After all, he had to point out her own culpability, but until then...

The sight of an oil smear on his last clean shirt reminded him of something else. Coming to a sudden decision, he told Anna quietly, 'I need to go home for...for a few days—check my post, make a few phone calls...'

'Oh, yes, of course...'

Even though she tried hard to conceal it Anna knew that her feelings must be showing on her face. She hated the thought of being without him and she knew she would miss him dreadfully.

'I'd like you to come with me,' Ward added quickly.

'Go with you...?' Anna's eyes widened. 'But what about Missie and Whittaker?'

'They can come too,' Ward assured her.

Go with him. See his house. Perhaps meet his friends... Anna's heart gave a small skip of pleasure.

'Oh, Ward, yes, I'd love to.' She beamed happily.

* * *

'What's all this about Anna and this man she's got staying with her?' Kelly asked Beth curiously.

'What man? I don't know what you're talking about,'
Beth replied as she stared incredulously at her friend
and partner. 'It can't possibly be true... We'd have
known. Anna would have told us. Besides, she just
isn't...she just doesn't...'

Beth paused and looked at Kelly.

'She just isn't like that.'

Kelly knew exactly what Beth meant. It wasn't that
Anna wasn't a desirable or attractive woman—she
was—but there was an air of shyness about her, an air
of...of purity, for want of a better word. Kelly acknowledged that that made it hard to imagine her even flirting
with a man, never mind letting one move in with her.

'There must be a mistake,' Beth protested uneasily.

'Not according to Mary Charles. Apparently she saw
him up at the house when she went to see Anna and
Anna actually introduced him to her as her "friend."'

The two young women eyed one another specula-
tively.

'Dee might know,' Beth volunteered. 'She and Anna
have become quite close recently.'

'Dee *might* know,' Kelly agreed, 'but she's in
Northumberland with her aunt.'

'Oh, yes, of course; I'd forgotten.'

Kelly gave Beth a thoughtful look. Beth had become
increasingly remote and preoccupied recently, and if
Kelly hadn't known better she would almost have imagined Beth was concealing something from her. But Beth
simply wasn't that type, just as her godmother wasn't
the type to have a live-in man 'friend.'

'Do you think one of us should go up and see Anna?'
Beth asked eventually.

Kelly pursed her lips.

'Well, of course, Anna's private life is really none of our business. However… I'll have a word with Brough and see what he thinks,' she offered.

'Mmm…Brough will know what to do,' Beth agreed.

Her godmother wasn't a wealthy woman but she wasn't a poor one either and, as Beth knew to her cost, there *were* men around who were all too eager to take advantage of a vulnerable woman. Look at the way she had deceived herself over Julian Cox, letting herself be persuaded that he loved her when all he had really been interested in was the money he'd thought she was going to inherit.

Mind you, she had certainly learned her lesson there and she would certainly *never* make that mistake again. The best way to treat men was with the same lack of real emotion with which they treated women. There was, after all, nothing morally wrong about enjoying sex for its own sake, about using a man in the same way that men used women… Beth gave a small toss of her head. No, there was nothing wrong with that at all, despite what a certain person seemed to think.

'Beth, come back,' Kelly commanded her friend wryly.

Flushing a little guiltily, Beth collected her thoughts. 'Mary is bound to have got it wrong,' she told Kelly. 'The man she saw was probably just a friend of Anna's.'

'Mmm… I expect you're right,' Kelly agreed.

'Brough, I'm worried about Anna.'

Brough looked up from the papers he had been reading to study Kelly's concerned face.

'Why, what's wrong with her?' he asked her calmly. 'If she's not well…'

'No, it isn't anything like that,' Kelly told him quickly, shaking her head. 'It's…well, she's disappeared, Brough, and no one seems to know where she's gone. I went up to the house yesterday. It's all closed up. There was no sign of her, or of Missie or Whittaker either.'

'Perhaps she's decided to have a holiday,' Brough suggested reasonably, but Kelly shook her head even harder.

'No, not without telling someone. Oh, I wish that Dee was here,' she told him fretfully.

'Have you asked Beth if she knows anything?' Brough asked her.

'She doesn't,' Kelly informed him. 'Not that there's much point in trying to discuss anything with Beth these days. She seems to be living in a world of her own. Something happened to her in Prague,' she stated positively, briefly switching her thoughts from Anna's disappearance to Beth's unusual behaviour. 'But I don't know what and every time I try to get her to open up to me she shuts me out. She's worrying about something, I can tell.

'Oh, Brough, I'm so worried about Anna. It just isn't like her to disappear like that without telling anyone.'

Brough put down his papers and walked over to her, her distress making him frown a little.

'She's run her own life ever since she was widowed, Kelly,' he told her gently.

'Yes, I know that, and I know what you're thinking as well,' Kelly informed him accusingly. 'You think I'm being irrational and over-emotional. Well, perhaps I am a little, but, Brough, I can't help worrying.'

She paused and then looked at him before announcing, 'Julian Cox has disappeared as well.'

As she saw the look of angry distaste that crossed her fiancé's face, Kelly wished that she hadn't had to bring up the subject of Julian Cox. Brough had every reason to dislike the other man—they both did—and normally he was the last person Kelly would have wanted to talk about—after all, he had nearly destroyed their love—but her concern for her friend overrode her natural inclination to avoid the subject.

'I heard it in town and Harry confirmed it. It seems he left town whilst we were away, without any kind of warning, leaving all manner of debts behind him. No one has the least idea where he's gone.'

'The further the better so far as I'm concerned,' Brough told her grimly.

Harry was his sister Eve's fiancé and cousin to Dee.

It had been Dee who had been instrumental in bringing Brough and Kelly together, and because of that Brough had decided to overlook her other and far less beneficial manipulation of people and events in her determination to win the war she was waging against Julian Cox.

'Brough, you don't think that Anna's disappearance has anything to do with Julian, do you?' Kelly asked him uncertainly.

Brough's eyebrows lifted. 'Surely you aren't suggesting that Anna's fallen for him, in view of what she knows about him—'

'Of course not.' Kelly interrupted him impatiently. 'I didn't mean that at all.' She looked serious. 'What I meant was, what if…?' She stopped, unable to put into words her frightening suspicions.

'Brough,' she whispered, her throat dry, 'what if he

made her go with him? You know how desperate he was for money.'

'But surely Anna isn't *that* wealthy? I know she's comfortably off, but—Kelly, what is it?' he demanded sternly. 'There's something you aren't telling me, isn't there?'

Kelly was torn between her loyalty to her friend and her concern for her. In the end her concern and Brough's seriousness won.

'Dee and Anna were trying to trap Julian into betraying himself. He'd hinted to Anna in the past about needing a loan, so… Well, to cut a long story short, Anna let him believe that she had quite a large sum of money she wanted to invest…'

There was an ominous silence before Brough said quietly, 'I see. Well, that puts an entirely different complexion on the matter. Have you spoken to Dee about Anna's disappearance?'

Kelly shook her head.

'No. She's in Northumberland.'

'Hmm… You know, it seems to me, Kelly, that there's far more behind Dee's desire to punish Julian Cox than she's ever revealed to the rest of you.'

'Yes, I think you're right,' Kelly agreed. 'I've often wondered myself, but…'

'She's never given you any hint?'

'No, nothing. In fact—well, Dee isn't the kind of person who encourages you to ask personal questions. I did wonder initially if at some stage Dee might have fallen for him herself, but I just can't see it.'

'No, neither can I,' Brough agreed.

'Perhaps Harry might know something; after all, he is Dee's cousin.'

'Well, he might, but what's more important right now

is finding out exactly what's happened to Anna. Who else is likely to know where she could have gone, apart from Beth?'

'Well, either Dee or yourself—but there's still something I haven't told you, Brough. When Mary Charles went to see Anna recently, there was a man there with her.'

'A man?' Brough gave her a blank look.

'Yes. Mary seemed to think... Well, apparently Anna introduced him to her as a "friend."'

'A friend...?' Brough looked blank and a little irritated. 'What does *that* mean?'

'I mean friend with a capital F. Which means...'

Kelly stopped. What was the point of trying to explain the nuances of female conversation to her fiancé— a mere man? Brough wasn't listening anyway. Instead he was asking her, 'Did this...this Mary Charles say what this man's name was? If she did, we could get in touch with him and check if he knows anything about Anna's disappearance.'

'Well, yes and no. She says that Anna introduced him to her as Ward but that she didn't give his surname.'

'Oh, that's very helpful.' Brough looked exasperated. 'You do realise, don't you, that if Anna is having a...relationship with this man, this Ward, whoever he may be, she might have her own reasons for choosing not to discuss it or him with any of you?'

'If that was the case she wouldn't have introduced him to Mary, would she?' Kelly countered, and then added, 'Besides, that's just not Anna; she isn't like that. She's shy, Brough, and...and cautious. I really am worried about her,' Kelly told him quietly. 'We both know how...how violent Julian can be. If something went

wrong and he discovered that Dee and Anna were trying
to trap him…'

'Mmm… Well, the first thing we should do is to get
in touch with Dee and find out if *she* knows anything
about Anna's plans and this unknown friend of hers.'

'I thought you said you lived in an old farmhouse,'
Anna gasped as Ward brought his car to a halt in the
courtyard of the stone-built building which was both far
larger and far more formidable than Anna had visual-
ised.

'It is—or rather it was,' Ward told her.

It looked more like a cross between a manor house
and a small fortress, Anna decided as Ward opened the
car door for her, and even inside the enclosed courtyard
the air was noticeably cooler than it had been back in
Rye.

When she said as much to Ward, he reasoned dryly,
'That's because we're several hundred metres higher
here. The house was built originally by a family of rich
wool merchants from York. It had been left empty for
several years before I bought it.'

'It's rather isolated,' Anna felt bound to point out.

They had driven for what had seemed like miles
through empty countryside, climbing all the time, before
reaching their destination, but Anna had to admit there
was something bracing and exhilarating about the wide
emptiness of the sky above them and the rolling landscape of the Dales around them.

'Well, it certainly doesn't encourage casual visitors,'
Ward agreed, and Anna could tell that he considered
that an advantage.

If it had been her home she would have softened the
austerity of the courtyard with tubs of plants and wall

baskets, Anna decided as she waited for Ward to re-
trieve her case from the boot of his car.

'This way,' he instructed her, leading the way to a
heavy and very old oak door.

The passage it opened onto was narrow and dark,
stone-flagged and icy cold. Anna shivered as she waited
for Ward to switch on the light. When he did she could
see that, whilst the walls and the floor were meticu-
lously clean, they presented an appearance of unwel-
coming austerity. Only one door led off the passage into
a large, well-equipped kitchen. Anna looked with relief
at the well-made wooden units and the large burgundy
Aga. The room was large enough to hold a good-sized
oak table and the stone floor had been softened by a
couple of rag rugs.

'This is lovely,' she told Ward appreciatively.

'My mother's choice,' Ward informed her. 'She said
I'd never get anyone up here to cook or clean for me
if I didn't provide them with a decent kitchen.

'I'll show you over the house and then we'd better
have something to eat.'

They had stopped for a snack on the way to
Yorkshire but Anna had been too excited at the thought
of seeing Ward's home to eat very much.

Half an hour later her excitement had faded, to be
replaced by a mixture of complex emotions. Seeing
Ward's house—she could not call it a home—had almost been like studying a blank canvas. None of the
rooms Ward had shown her, not even his own bedroom,
betrayed anything of his character. Even the room
where he worked was as austere as the rest of the house.

There was nothing wrong with the house itself. Its
rooms were well proportioned, its views awesomely
stunning, the furniture sparse but of good quality. It was

just that the house was so sterile. It had no life, no warmth…no heart, and as she looked at Ward Anna suddenly felt unbearably sad for him. The house was so…so loveless. Had it been hers…

Anna allowed herself to daydream for a few minutes. That huge master bedroom he had shown her needed softening with fabrics that were sympathetic to the age and character of the house, not pretty chintzes, of course, but there were other fabrics—damasks, rich velvets in ruby-reds, imperial blues, warm golds, cool linens in sky-blues and watery greens—that would complement the landscape.

The single ceiling lights needed replacing with lamps and wall lights. The large plain white bathroom needed thick, fluffy towels. The dull brown carpet needed replacing with something lighter and richer. The big double bed needed a rich, dramatic cover; the sofas in the television and drawing rooms needed heaping with piles of cushions. The bare walls cried out for paintings, the empty surfaces of the furniture for bowls of flowers and family photographs.

Family photographs!

That was what this house needed, what it lacked. It lacked a family. It lacked love, as perhaps Ward had lacked it before they had met one another. A huge lump filled Anna's throat. She loved him so much, ached for him so much. She only had to see this house to know that there must have been a time in his life when he had felt very unloved.

As Ward watched the expressions chasing one another over Anna's face, he realised that he had seen them before. His mother's eyes had held that same look of loving compassion when she had gently tried to persuade him to move closer to her and his stepfather.

'I like it here,' he had told her stubbornly.

'But, darling, it's so…so bleak,' she had sighed.

Ward had shrugged away her criticism. It might seem bleak to her. To him it felt merely private, secure…safe.

'I'll take your things up and put them in the guest room; it's got its own *en suite* bathroom and if you want to have Missie and Whittaker up there with you…'

The spare guest bedroom. Anna looked at him in surprise. She had naturally assumed that she would be sharing *his* room, *his* bed.

Ward could see what she was thinking but this time he was prepared. He had had the long drive north to think about the situation and he had decided what he must do—and say.

'Ecclestone is a bit old-fashioned,' he told her, 'and I wouldn't want Mrs Jarvis to get the wrong idea about our relationship.'

It was, after all, the truth. He certainly didn't want his cleaner carrying tales back to the town that he and Anna were a couple. His mother still had contacts in the area, and sooner or later the news would get to her ear, and when it did…

It was no secret to Ward that his mother very much wanted him to marry again and have a family—not for her sake, as she was always quick to reassure him whenever she raised the subject, which was virtually every time she saw him, but for his own. If she thought for one moment that there was a woman in his life she would move heaven and earth to keep her there—permanently!

It was, though, also true that Ward did not relish the thought of being the subject of local gossip. He had endured enough of that when his marriage had broken up. But that, of course, was not the real reason why he wanted them to have separate bedrooms!

It was sweet of Ward to want to be so protective and chivalrous, Anna acknowledged, but she would still rather…

'We are both mature adults,' she reminded him gently. 'And both free to…to choose what we do with our lives.' She looked at Ward gravely but she could sense that he wasn't going to change his mind.

It would, she knew, be relatively easy to persuade him to change it. If she went over to him now, for instance, and started to coax him, touch him, *seduce* him… But she simply wasn't that kind of woman. She wanted Ward to want her, to be proud of desiring her, to want her love so recklessly that he simply didn't care what other people thought. And, after all, if he really felt so strongly about other people's views and about her, then he could always ensure that no one had any reason to gossip about them. There was nothing to stop them from making public vows of the commitment they had surely already made to one another privately.

Maybe they had not known one another very long, but it must be long enough for Anna to be very sure of *her* feelings, long enough for her to know that if Ward were to ask her to marry him she would say yes.

'What would you like to do tomorrow? We still haven't been to Lindisfarne, and then there's—'

'Couldn't we just stay here?' Anna asked Ward gently. She had been in Yorkshire for three days now and every day Ward had insisted on taking her out.

They had spent a day in York, which she had loved, and another in Harrogate. Ward had driven her miles through the Dales, delighting her both with his knowl-

edge of his home county and the sights he had shown
her. They had eaten magnificent Yorkshire high teas in
York and in Harrogate's famous tea shop, and delicious
lunches in traditional village pubs in the small Dales
villages, sumptuous dinners in restaurants boasting
many prestigious awards. But all Anna really longed for
was to be alone with Ward, with a simple meal of nothing more exotic than bread and cheese washed down
with a bottle of wine, and with the knowledge that he
wanted and loved her. That was what she wanted.

Yesterday, after a delicious lunch, they had walked,
climbing the moorland track until they found a sheltered
spot to rest surrounded by empty moorland and out of
sight of any curious eyes. Anna had longed for Ward
to take hold of her, kiss her, make love with her, the
way he had done in Rye, and for a second she had
thought he would. She had stumbled on a piece of stone
and he had reached out to steady her, asking, 'Are you
all right?'

When she had nodded she had seen the way his gaze
slid to her mouth and stayed there. Her heart had started
thumping, her body quivering with longing for him. He
had moved closer towards her so that she could feel the
warmth of his body, and her mouth had become dry
with arousal and tension. Automatically she had licked
her lips. Immediately Ward had released her, turning
away from her, but as he had done so she had thought
she heard him groan.

Now Anna longed for the courage to be bolder, to be
able to express her longing for him openly, but it simply
wasn't her nature. She was finding her loss of memory
increasingly frustrating; without any proper knowledge
of the history of her relationship with Ward to guide

her she had no idea how to deal with the present situation.

He didn't want people to gossip about them, he had told her, and, naturally, it had pleased her that he should be concerned for her reputation, but she was beginning to feel as though their relationship existed in some kind of vacuum. It had no past, or at least none that *she* could remember, nor did it seem to have any future, or at least not one which Ward wanted to discuss with her.

Anna shook her head, trying to disperse her uncomfortable thoughts. Perhaps it was the bad dreams she had been having these past two nights that were making her feel so on edge and uneasy. None of her dreams seemed to make any sense; they were a confusing mixture of images, faces, scraps of conversation, untidily woven together with her own emotions of despair, fear and anger. In them she could hear Ward's voice, raised and angry, but the words he was speaking to her made no sense, nor did her frantic anxiety over money, her desperate physical searching for it.

All in all, Anna was beginning to question whether she had made the right decision in agreeing to come north with Ward.

Turning his back on Anna, Ward walked over to the sink and looked out of the window. His heart was thumping heavily, too heavily; keeping Anna at arm's length was proving even more difficult than he had imagined.

Yesterday on the fell he had been so tempted to take her in his arms and kiss her, so very, very tempted, and he had seen from the baffled, hurt expression in her eyes that she couldn't understand why he had not done so.

He was growing tired of having to remind himself

just why he had brought her here. After all, what was five thousand pounds to him? He could easily afford to lose ten times that amount of money. It was his own stiff-necked pride that had brought him to this impasse. If he hadn't been so determined to make her repay Ritchie, he wouldn't be in this situation now.

If he had any sense he would get the car out and drive her home right now. After all, she had friends, a god-daughter, who could look after her until she recovered her memory. It wasn't *his* responsibility to take care of her. What did he actually owe her? Nothing. *She* was the one who owed *him*...five thousand pounds.

But, despite the logic of his thoughts, Ward knew that he did have an obligation towards her. He should never have allowed her to believe that they were lovers and, if he hadn't been so furiously angry with her, so determined to make her admit that she had lied to him when she had denied being Julian Cox's partner, he would never have done so. His own deceit was going to cost him an awful lot more than a mere five thousand pounds. It was going to cost him a lifetime of pain and guilt and regret, Ward acknowledged.

'Ward?'

He stiffened as he heard Anna's voice directly behind him. Anna took a deep breath as she waited for him to turn round. She knew what she had to say, what her pride demanded that she say, but that wasn't going to make it any easier.

'Ward, I think it's time I went home,' she announced quietly.

Somehow Ward managed to suppress his instinctive cry of denial, his instinctive refusal to allow her to go...to leave him.

'Very well,' he heard himself saying harshly. 'If that's what you want.'

'It is,' Anna lied.

Through the kitchen window she could see the courtyard. It was raining, a dull, steady downpour from clouds which had masked the tops of the hills she could see from her bedroom, cloaking the landscape in mist.

'I'll go upstairs and pack,' she added, stepping away from Ward and turning her back to him.

'The car needs petrol; I'll go down into town and fill the tank whilst you're packing,' Ward told her shortly.

Anything, anything, to put a safe distance between them. If he stayed, he knew he wouldn't be able to stop himself from begging her to change her mind.

They were treating one another like strangers, Anna thought despairingly as he picked up his keys and headed for the door. But then, in many ways, wasn't that what he was to her? A stranger and her lover. But he hadn't been her lover these last few nights. He had kept her at a distance, in a separate room.

Her case was packed but Ward still hadn't returned. Anna tutted as Whittaker jumped out of her arms and through the open door into Ward's study.

Irritably she followed him inside, calling him back. There were some papers on Ward's desk. He had been working the previous evening after their return from dinner. He had been in a quiet mood all evening, uncommunicative with her, and distant, and eventually she had gone to bed without interrupting him.

Whittaker jumped up onto Ward's desk, refusing to come to her. Tiredly Anna scolded him as he sat down on Ward's papers.

'You are a bad cat,' she told him ruefully as she

leaned across the desk to pick him up. Absently she glanced at the papers he had been seated on, more to check that he hadn't left them covered in paw-prints than for any other reason, then she froze as a name leapt off the printed page in front of her.

Julian Cox!

Anna ignored Whittaker's miaow of protest as she gripped him tightly. The room spun round her, going dark, dissolving in a terrifying vortex of fractured images and memories.

Julian Cox.

She could see him, hear his voice. She started to tremble with reaction and fear. She had lost Dee's money to him, her fifty thousand pounds. He had frightened her with his constant phone calls, asking her when he could have the money she was supposed to be investing with him. There had been something almost unbalanced and dangerous about him, as though he was a man close to going totally out of control.

Anna had wanted to tell Dee how she felt but she hadn't wanted to let her down, so she had suppressed her anxiety, with disastrous results. Perhaps if she had spoken up Dee would still have her money.

The black mist was starting to clear, Whittaker's plaintive miaows bringing her back to reality. What she had just experienced had been a flashback and resurgence of her missing memory, Anna recognised as her body shook with cold and reaction. Her skin felt clammy, drenched with an icy sweat; she felt nauseous and her head ached.

Julian Cox.

She could remember now, but what had he to do with Ward? It was like lifting the newly formed scab off a vicious wound, opening the door to a dark cellar, know-

ing that what lay as yet unseen was something poten-
tially threatening and frightening.

Anna forced herself to look a second time at the paper on Ward's desk, and this time she deliberately read
it.

When she had finished, her face was chalk white.

It was a report on Julian Cox and her as co-partners
in an investment company.

Totally in shock, Anna walked into the kitchen,
Whittaker following at her heels. Beside the Aga Missie
was curled up in her basket. She jumped up as her mistress walked in and raced to the back door.

Walk time!

Anna stared at her blank-eyed and then automatically
opened the door, following Missie out into the courtyard
and then beyond it.

It was still raining but Anna neither noticed nor cared
as she followed Missie up the steep hillside; she was
totally absorbed in the traumatic chaos of her thoughts
and the return of her memory.

She and Ward weren't really lovers at all. He had
come to see her, claiming that she had cheated his
brother out of money. Anna could remember it all.

The path she was following climbed steeply; her
clothes, her hair, her skin were drenched in rain, but she
scarcely noticed. All around her the landscape was now
clothed in a wet white mist, but Anna trudged on, placing one foot in front of the other like an automaton.

Ward didn't love her—he didn't even like her; but
he had gone to bed with her, let her think...let her believe... Anna bit back the anguished sound that bubbled
in her throat.

Oh, God, why? Why had he done it? To punish her,
hurt her. Anna felt sick with shock and disbelief. Up

ahead of her Missie barked and a startled rabbit suddenly shot across the path virtually under her feet, almost causing her to stumble.

Anna called out to her dog as she raced after the rabbit, but Missie ignored her, her small white body quickly melting into the surrounding mist-covered landscape.

Anna's teeth started to chatter. It was almost impossible to believe it was summer, she felt so cold.

She called out to Missie again and then waited, listening, but all she could hear was the anxious thudding of her own heartbeat. A patch of slightly thicker mist caught her eye; swiftly she walked towards it, letting out a small protest of dismay when it dispersed without revealing her errant dog.

'Missie,' Anna called again, and was rewarded with an excited bark.

Thankfully, she turned towards the sound. She had lost the path now, and the hillside beneath her feet was rough with tussocks of grass and boulders. She almost stumbled on one of them but managed to save herself just in time, wincing as she realised that she had scraped the hand she had put out to prevent herself from falling.

'Missie,' she cried out anxiously, hearing the sound of her own voice bounce back to her in the mist.

This was crazy. She couldn't possibly be more than a few minutes from the house, but she couldn't see further than a few inches in front of her nose and she couldn't recognise anything either. It made sense that if she went uphill she would be going further away and if she went down she had to be going back.

Half an hour later, her hands and clothes muddy from a series of stumbles, her heart pounding and her legs aching, Anna acknowledged that she had absolutely no

idea where she was. Logically she ought to have
reached the house long ago, but no matter how hard she
tried to pierce the gloom of the mist all she could see
was mist. A darker shadow suddenly loomed out of the
hillside, making her scream in fright until she realised
it was only a sheep—a sheep hotly followed by Missie.

'Oh, Missie.' She scolded the little dog in relief.
'Where have you been, you naughty dog?'

She had a terrible pain in her head, a knife-like ache
that was making her feel sick and dizzy. Missie wriggled in her arms and broke free.

Anna called to her to come back. She had to sit down,
her legs felt so shaky and weak. The grass felt wet, but
no wetter than her damp clothes. She was cold as well,
but the cold on the outside of her body was no worse
than the dreadful icy chill inside it.

How could Ward have done that to her?

Anna closed her eyes, trying to put her chaotic
thoughts into some kind of order. She could remember
that first meeting with him quite clearly—his anger,
their argument. She could remember, too, seeing him
again in the hospital. A low moan of pain escaped her
as she recalled what she had said to him.

How *could* she have done that? What on earth had
possessed her?

But he hadn't corrected her. He had let her... Oh, the
exquisite memory of what she had believed—how he
must have relished it, knowing the humiliation that lay
ahead of her once she regained her memory—the self-
inflicted humiliation.

Dry-eyed, Anna stared into the mist. She was lost and
alone but she didn't care. She didn't care if no one ever
found her. In fact, she decided, it would be far better if
they didn't. How on earth was she going to face people

now? How on earth was she going to face *Ward*? She had humiliated herself utterly and completely—and he had let her. And she had thought him so wonderful, so caring, so upright and honest.

Anna started to laugh, a wild, high-pitched sound, only partially muffled by the thickening mist.

CHAPTER NINE

WARD had been gone much longer than he had planned. He had bumped into an old friend of his mother's in the garage, an elderly widow who had been having an anxious discussion with the mechanic about the state of her small car.

Automatically Ward had gone to see if she needed any help. It had turned out that the mechanic was trying to explain to her just why he considered her small car to be unfit to drive, but, as she had explained tearfully to Ward, she couldn't manage without it nor afford to replace it.

After soothing her over tea in a nearby café, Ward had driven her home. He had then gone back to the garage where he had questioned the mechanic and given him certain instructions. After he had gone, the mechanic had shaken his head and told the apprentice, 'Weird guy. He only wants me to replace that Mini with the one we've got for sale—and he's paid cash for it— but he wants us to re-spray it the same colour as the other one. I warned him what it would cost but—' he gave a brief shrug '—he said he wasn't concerned about the cost… Like I said—weird…'

Ward had his apology and his explanation ready for Anna as he drove into the courtyard, but she wasn't, as he had expected, waiting for him in the kitchen, annoyed by his tardiness. Her cat was there, though. Ward stroked him absently as he walked past him and into the hallway.

His study door was open, the report he had been reading the previous night still on his desk. He went in and picked it up. Last night he had made himself re-read it just to remind himself of exactly what Anna was, but it hadn't worked. He had still gone to bed aching for her, longing for her, missing the soft, sweet weight of her in his arms. How was it possible for him to feel like that in such a short space of time, to miss her so intensely in his bed that he was constantly waking up, searching for her? It had been less than a fortnight since he had first met her, for God's sake.

Less than a fortnight, hardly more than a week. No time at all, but more than time enough to change his whole life.

Abruptly he picked up the report, tore it in half and then in half again, needing an outlet for the anger he could feel building up inside him.

The house felt quiet and still…empty…just the way he liked it—just the way he *used* to like it! He called out Anna's name sharply, warned by some prescient instinct even before he had taken the stairs two at a time and pushed open her bedroom door to discover her suitcase but no Anna.

It took him less than ten minutes to search the house from top to bottom.

No sign of her. So where was she?

In the kitchen the cat was lying triumphantly in Missie's basket. Ward frowned. Where was Missie?

He glanced through the window, his heart starting to thud.

Surely Anna hadn't taken her out for a walk in this?

He raced back into the courtyard calling both Anna and Missie's names as he pulled on a thick waterproof country jacket.

She must surely have recognised how dangerous it was to walk *anywhere* in this mist. Even he, who knew the hills around here like the back of his hand, would have thought twice. It was the easiest thing in the world to get lost...

He found Missie first. She came flying towards him out of the mist, barking excitedly, flinging herself at him. She was wet and her white coat matted with mud.

Ward hugged her fiercely.

'Where is she, Missie?' he demanded thickly. 'Where's Anna? Where is she...?'

When he put her down Missie stared at him and wagged her tail.

'Where is she, Missie?' Ward begged. 'Find Anna. Find her.'

The dog ran off uncertainly and then ran back to him.

Ward's heart sank. Anna could be anywhere out there. Anywhere.

'Anna... Anna...' He cupped his hands together and called her name.

And then he heard it, the eerie, almost inhuman sound of someone laughing, so faint that at first he thought he must have imagined it.

Straining his ears, he listened, hurrying as fast as he dared in the direction of the faint sound.

'Anna! Anna!'

Silence.

Ward cursed. At his feet Missie whined and then barked excitedly. Ward tensed hopefully, but she was only barking at a stray sheep.

'No,' he told her sternly as she made to chase it, but Missie wasn't listening to him.

'Missie,' he called as she ran off, then plunged into the thick mist behind her, cursing her under his breath.

She was barking again, having no doubt caught up with the lumbering sheep. Ward could just about make out the shape of her up ahead of him. He hurried after her and then stopped abruptly as he saw why she had stopped.

Anna was sitting there on the hillside, looking as calm and unruffled as though she were sitting in the kitchen of her own home.

'Anna!'

'Hello, Ward,' she greeted him quietly.

'Anna!'

Relief poured through him as Ward hurried up to her.

'What are you doing? What happened? Are you all right?'

In his anxiety Ward didn't notice the way Anna was gripping her hands together to control the way she was shaking. She had heard him calling out to her and she had known that sooner or later he would find her and that once he did... But her head ached so much, *hurt* so much, that there was no way she could even think about what she ought to say to him. It was so much easier simply to say nothing, simply to let him take charge and urge her to her feet whilst he demanded to know why on earth she had gone for a walk in such dangerous conditions.

'I didn't realise,' she told him emotionlessly. 'I followed Missie...'

Her eyes felt heavy and she wanted to close them. She started to shiver violently.

Her body felt like ice but her face was flushed—almost feverishly so, Ward recognised in concern as he guided her carefully back towards the path.

'Are you sure you're all right?' Ward demanded anxiously once they were back in the farmhouse kitchen.

'You don't look well. Perhaps I should get a doctor out…'

'No,' Anna responded sharply. 'No. I'm fine… Besides, we're leaving anyway, aren't we?'

'Leaving?' Ward looked at her grimly. 'Not until you've had a hot bath and something to eat, we aren't,' he told her firmly.

'I've packed all my clothes,' Anna objected.

'Then I'll *un*pack some for you,' Ward told her, adding sternly, 'You're soaking wet, Anna; you can't go anywhere like that.'

Ward was growing increasingly concerned about her. She seemed so cold and distant, so unlike her normal warm, loving self. He should never have left her alone for so long. Anything could have happened to her out there on the moors. As it was, she would be lucky if she didn't end up with a severe cold, if not something worse, and it would all be his fault.

Anna started to shiver convulsively. Ward cursed under his breath, sweeping her up into his arms.

'What are you doing? Put me down,' Anna objected, but Ward refused to listen to her.

The *en suite* bathroom off his own room had a huge whirlpool bath, which his mother had persuaded him to install.

'They're wonderful for rheumatism,' she had told him.

'But I don't *have* rheumatism,' Ward had pointed out.

'Not yet,' she had agreed. 'But you aren't getting any younger, you know, Ward.'

It had been a dig at the fact that he wasn't married, that he hadn't provided her with any grandchildren; Ward knew that but he had still installed the bath. Not that he often used it. He preferred to shower, but right now he was mentally blessing his mother for her inter-ference as he kicked the bathroom door shut behind him and carefully placed Anna down on her feet.

'Ward…' Anna began to protest as he started to run the bath and fill it with hot water.

But then she stopped speaking as she was seized by another violent fit of shivers that made her teeth chatter. Ward had rolled up the sleeves of his shirt to fill the bath and Anna noticed distantly how the light glinted on the soft fine hair on his arms. He was such a mas-culine man, such a *male* man, and she had felt so very, very safe in his arms. She gave a small sob and closed her eyes, only to open them again as she felt Ward's hands on her body, tugging at her clothes.

'Anna, for heaven's sake,' Ward protested as she started to push him away.

'I can undress myself,' she told him fiercely. 'I will undress myself,' she added pointedly. 'When you've gone…'

Ward wasn't going to argue. She was behaving very oddly, but the longer she stood there in her soaking wet clothes the greater her chances of becoming ill.

Shrugging, he walked past her and opened the bath-room door.

Anna waited until he had closed it behind him before inspecting it. No lock. Her lips tightened, her eyes sud-denly bleak. She wasn't really afraid that he was going to come back or try to force himself on her. After all, he had had the opportunity to have as much sex with her as he could have wanted these last few days and he had totally ignored her. She gave a bitter, mirthless smile.

Was there no end to her humiliation at his hands?

First he encouraged her to betray herself to him in the
most intimate way possible and then he rejected her.

Bitterly she tugged off her clothes and then stepped
into the hot water, gasping a little as its heat touched
her icy cold skin. The bath really was huge, easily large
enough for two people, even when one of them was as
big as Ward.

Ward!

Anna closed her eyes as two tears dripped down her
face. Angrily she reached for the button that turned on
the bath's water jets. What was she crying for? She
hated him…hated him…

'Anna…?'

Ward paused outside the closed bathroom door as he
called Anna's name. No reply. Anxiously he opened the
door and then stopped.

Anna was curled up on the bathroom floor, fast
asleep, wrapped in a towel. With her hair damp and her
face free of make-up she looked so young, so vulnerable, so…so lovable.

His throat raw with emotion, Ward leaned down and
picked her up. Sleepily she opened her eyes and whispered drowsily, 'Ward…'

'Shush, it's all right. Go back to sleep,' Ward told
her gently as he carried her through to the bedroom and
placed her on his bed. Carefully tucking the duvet round
her, Ward faced the truth. He loved her and there was
no way he could ever let her go. No matter what she
might have done. It was so odd, but now that his fight
to deny how he felt about her was over and he had lost
he actually felt almost euphoric with relief, as though a
huge weight had been lifted from his shoulders.

What he was thinking, feeling, planning was contrary

to everything he had always believed in, and yet all he could feel was a tremendous surge of joy that he was finally free to admit his love for her.

Once he was sure she was comfortable he went back downstairs. Missie and Whittaker still had to be fed and he had some work he might as well do whilst he waited for Anna to wake up.

For the rest of the day Anna drifted in and out of an uneasy sleep. Several times Ward went up to check on her, reluctant to wake her but anxiously checking her skin and her pulse just in case she had a temperature.

He ate a solitary evening meal. Outside the mist had started to lift. The house was quiet but not empty. Not any longer, not any more.

Humming lightly to himself, Ward went upstairs again. Anna woke up as the bed depressed beneath Ward's weight when he got in beside her.

'Ward.'

'Mmm…' he acknowledged as he reached for her, wrapping his arms tightly around her as he drew her down against his body—his very male and totally naked body, Anna recognised in shock. She wanted to tell him not to touch her, not to lie to her and deceive her, but Ward had already started to kiss her, gently at first and with such false tenderness that her eyes filled with tears.

'Don't cry, don't cry,' she heard him whisper softly. 'You're safe here with me, Anna. You're safe now. Everything's all right…'

Everything *wasn't* all right. Anna knew that, but her body was turning traitor on her and Ward's kisses were growing increasingly intense and passionate.

She tried to resist him and she might have succeeded, but she couldn't resist *herself*. She wanted him so…loved him so… Her heart gave a painful jolt against her ribs.

'You're shivering,' Ward told her huskily. 'Are you cold? How do you feel? Are you all right?'

Anna knew that she wasn't shivering, she was *trembling*, and the cause of her tremors wasn't any residual cold from being trapped on the misty hillside but something much more immediate and personal. In fact, the cause of them was lying right beside her, holding her, stroking her arms with pseudo-tender, caring little caresses as though he wanted to comfort her with his own body heat. What was it about men that allowed them to behave so differently from women? He didn't love her, didn't even *like* her, and *he* certainly wasn't blinded to the truth by any amnesia, and yet here he was, holding her, touching her, making love with her as though…as though…

Only her pride prevented Anna from blurting out that she had regained her memory; that she knew everything. Her pride and the sure knowledge that if she did so now the admission would be ignominiously accompanied by her tears, her anguish and pain that he should have treated her so callously and so cruelly. Surely, no matter what her supposed crime, to have done what Ward had done was a punishment far, far in excess of any true form of justice.

'Anna…'

Perhaps if she just closed her eyes and lay still he would stop touching her, withdraw from her and leave her alone. Anna knew that she couldn't trust her own voice to tell him that she didn't want him, and she certainly couldn't answer any of the questions he might try to ask her.

She didn't want him. Behind her closed eyelids Anna

felt her eyes burn with acidly bitter shaming tears. She couldn't lie to herself. She *did* want him. She wanted his tenderness, she wanted his touch, she wanted his *love*.

How could she, when everything he had allowed her to believe was a fiction?

Anna didn't know; all she *did* know was that her emotional response to him was so strong that it defied all logic. Her body, so sensitively attuned to his touch, was already responding to him and she simply didn't have the will-power to stop it.

And anyway, what was the point? she asked herself in aching resignation as he gently kissed her mouth, his hand slipping from her arm to her breast.

Why not add this one last memory to the others she already had? Why not *really* punish herself for her stupidity, her vulnerability, by giving in to the longing she could feel flooding her body like a form of sweetly venomous death?

With a small, painful sigh Anna turned towards Ward.

'Mmm...'

Bleakly she felt the warmth of his body enveloping her as he nuzzled the soft, tender flesh of her throat.

She put out a hand defensively. Beneath it she could feel the fine silk of his body hair. Her heart started to beat very fast; in a way it was almost as she had imagined drowning might be, easier to succumb, to give in than to try to fight feelings which only grew stronger with every breath she took.

'Oh, but I've missed you,' she heard Ward telling her throatily. 'These last few nights without you here, beside me.'

Anna forbore to mention that it had been *his* decision that they should sleep apart.

She gave an involuntary shudder as his thumb tip caressed her nipple... Immediately he bent his head and kissed it gently, and then less gently, until Anna was writhing achingly against him, powerless to stem the hot flood of feeling that roared through her like a forest fire. Her body, aware now of the pleasure he could give it, was way, way, beyond the control of her mind, her own desire, her own love a force that defied any kind of logic she tried to use to rein it in.

Instinctively she reached out to touch him, her body melting with pleasure as she felt his taut shudder of response. He might hate her, resent her, despise her, but he still wanted her. The savagely bitter shaft of acid pleasure that knowledge brought her told Anna just how destructive her feelings were, and as though to reinforce her own anger against herself she deliberately stroked her fingertips down the length of his body, touching him more boldly and more intimately than she had previously done without his own encouragement.

If she had expected Ward to stop her or withdraw himself from her she had been wrong. Instead he seemed to positively revel in the bold control she had taken of their lovemaking, groaning hoarsely deep in his throat, his eyes opening wide as he focused on her face.

'That feels so good,' he told her rawly. He was breathing heavily, his body filming with a light sweat that smelled mustily erotic. To Anna, who had always known she was almost a little too fastidious, the knowledge that her instinct was to bury her face against him and breathe in the pheromone-charged sensuality he was exuding was almost, in its way, more shocking than knowing how much she wanted him, how much her own disobedient, wanton body ached for the culmination of his lovemaking.

Beneath the soft pads of her fingertips his erection felt hard and muscular. Even without looking at him she knew how he would look, could remember the inexperienced awe with which she had first observed his body. Ralph's body had been that of a very young man, albeit firm and well-muscled. Ward possessed a much more raw and potent masculinity, a man fully grown in every sense of the word, Anna acknowledged as she explored and then caressed him with her fingers.

If so far in their 'relationship' she had taken from him a pleasure she had had no right to have, then now, tonight, she intended to repay *that* debt in full. Her sense of pride and honour demanded it.

In the darkness Ward moaned softly.

'I shouldn't be letting you do this,' he told her softly. 'I should be the one…'

'I *want* to do it,' Anna told him truthfully. This way at least she had some control over herself—and over him. What she didn't want to admit to herself was that there was a sharply sweet pleasure for her in what she was doing, in knowing she was giving him pleasure. Her own body was even reacting to it, responding to it, as though it too had been aroused and caressed.

'No, Anna, no more,' she heard Ward begging her gruffly as he took hold of her hand and gently removed it from himself, at the same time drawing her down against him and kissing her with open-mouthed passion.

Unable to stop herself from responding, Anna clung to him.

She wasn't sure which of them it was who was trembling the harder now, Ward or herself. She only knew that her body barely needed the assistance he gave it as he moulded it to his own, and it certainly needed neither coaxing nor teaching to accommodate the urgent thrust of his flesh against her own. If anything her body was even more sensitively responsive to him than it had been before, quickening, tightening even with his first eager movement into it. Somewhere, at the back of her mind, Anna knew she was in the very gravest danger and that it was wrong for her to feel so complete, so at one with a man with whom she could not possibly have any future. The beauty of what they were creating together was nothing more than a sham and deception. The agonised pleasure she could hear in Ward's voice was just another lie, like the love words he was whispering to her now as their bodies trembled in dizzy release.

'I love you, Anna,' he told her huskily as he cupped her face and kissed her. 'I love you.'

Anna waited until she was sure he was fast asleep before carefully sliding out of his bed. She knew what she had to do. Downstairs in the kitchen Whittaker and Missie were sleeping in their baskets and Ward's car keys were on the table. It was almost as though fate had at long last decided to help her.

Anna's final act after she had loaded her pets and her suitcase into Ward's car was to pull out her cheque book. Five thousand pounds was a lot of money to give away in payment of a debt she didn't even know about but it would be worth it. With the cheque she left a brief note:

'I've remembered everything. I shall leave your car at York station and post the keys back to you. This cheque repays the money you *believe* I owe your half-brother. Last night repays any debt I *might* have owed you.'

As she climbed into Ward's car and started it she blessed the manufacturer for its near-silent engine. There was no chance, of course, that Ward would come after her or try to get in touch with her.

All she had to face now was her friends at home. What a pity Mary Charles had had to call round when she had, but even harder to live with than her friends' curiosity would be her own shame and pain.

Ward woke up at first light, automatically reaching for Anna. When he discovered she wasn't there he waited for a few minutes, thinking initially she might be in the bathroom, and then, when there was no sign of her, he threw back the bedclothes and hurried downstairs.

He saw her note at the same time as he realised that the animals and their baskets had gone.

As he picked it up and read it, the blood left his face. His hand trembled as he picked up Anna's cheque, but it was the line she had written about repayment of any debt she might have owed him that he concentrated on most.

He glanced at the clock. Half past six. If she had driven to York that must mean she intended to go home by train. With a fast car he could be there before her. But he didn't have a fast car; he didn't have *any* car.

Cursing under his breath, he froze as the telephone rang abruptly. As he reached for the receiver his heart slammed fiercely against his chest. It could only be Anna; it had to be, ringing at this time. She must have realised, had a change of heart. But the tearful woman on the other end of the line wasn't Anna, it was his mother.

'Ward, it's Alfred; he's in hospital with a suspected heart attack. Oh, Ward, I'm so afraid for him.'

'Don't worry, Ma, I'll be with you as soon as I can,' Ward assured his mother.

He would have to ring the local taxi firm and get them to drive him to York. Where the hell were his spare car keys? In his desk drawer!

The last thing he did before he left the house was to tear up Anna's note—and her cheque.

CHAPTER TEN

'I TAKE it there's still no word from Anna?' Dee asked crisply. She and Beth and Kelly were seated upstairs in the flat above the shop. Dee had only arrived home late the previous evening in response to Kelly's anxious telephone call about Anna's disappearance.

'Nothing,' Beth responded.

With a wary look in Beth's direction Kelly asked uncertainly, 'Dee, do you think this man Mary saw her with *could* have anything to do with Julian Cox?'

'With Julian? Why should he have?' Beth asked sharply.

Warningly Dee shook her head at Kelly. They had agreed that there was no point in adding to the distress Beth had suffered over Julian's treatment of her by telling her what they had planned to do.

'Julian tried to borrow money from Anna,' Dee answered calmly. It was, after all, true.

Beth looked shocked.

'Oh, but surely that doesn't mean...' She stopped, and then whispered shakily, 'You don't really think that Julian might have done something to *hurt* Anna, do you?'

'He didn't think twice when it came to hurting you, did he?' Dee reminded her caustically.

'Does *anyone* know where he's gone?' Beth asked worriedly. She had hardly given Julian Cox a thought since her return from Prague. Her infatuation with him

145

and the pain he had caused her seemed unimportant now.

When was she going to hear from the factory about her crystal? She had invested far more than she could really afford in the consignment of crystal she had bought, recklessly almost quadrupling her original order, and she had used every spare bit of capital both she and Kelly had to pay for it in defiance of a warning to her that she would be well advised to give her business to the factory *he* had recommended to her. Did he *really* think she was so much of a fool? She'd known perfectly well that this man who'd been acting as her guide and interpreter was bound to be being paid by the factory owners—relatives of his—to direct potential business their way.

Her body tensed as she remembered how angry he had made her. Oh, but he had been so arrogant, so sure that he was right. She had been determined to show him that she didn't need his advice, that she was a modern, independent woman. People were often deceived into thinking that, because her nature was essentially so gentle, Beth could be pushed around, but beneath that gentleness she possessed a fortifying streak of stubbornness. Alex had challenged her and she had met that challenge—more than met it. But at what personal cost…?

'Beth!'

Guiltily she realised that Kelly was speaking to her and that she ought to be thinking about Anna and not her own problems.

'I agree that Julian has behaved very badly, but if Anna has disappeared—' She shook her head. 'No, I can't see him being involved in anything like that.'

Dee listened in silence. It was just as well that her

aunt had been virtually recovered when she'd got Kelly's phone call—she *had* been planning to return home later in the week anyway, and to come back a couple of days earlier hadn't been any problem.

Beth might believe that Julian couldn't be involved in Anna's disappearance but she didn't know him as well as Dee did, despite the fact that Beth and he had once been on the point of becoming engaged.

Julian had no regard for the feelings or the safety of others. His greed was such that he simply didn't care who he hurt and harmed, or how. Despite all the enquiries she had made whilst she had been staying with her aunt, she had found no evidence of Julian's whereabouts.

She had, at one stage, thought she had traced him as far as Hong Kong, which would make sense since she knew he had business dealings there, but if he was still there now there was certainly no official trace of him.

Could Anna have gone away with this mystery man Mary Charles had seen?

'She *could* have,' Beth answered, and Dee realised she had asked her question out loud. 'But why hasn't she told us about him if he is her lover? It's just so out of character for her—and we've only Mary Charles's word for it that they are—involved!'

'If he isn't her lover then who is he?' Kelly asked practically.

'The husband of one of her friends, perhaps?' Beth suggested, her forehead pleating in a small frown. 'Someone she had got round to do some work for her— a gardener or handyman, perhaps.'

'Mmm... Mary was adamant that when Anna introduced him to her as a ''friend'' she meant friend with a capital F.'

'Perhaps we *are* making too much fuss. Perhaps she just decided to go away for a few days without telling any of us,' Beth offered, but she knew she sounded as unconvinced as she felt. Guiltily, she remembered that when she had last spoken to her godmother on the telephone she had been impatient to end the call. Perhaps if she *hadn't* been Anna might have said something to her that would have given them some clue as to where she might be.

'Her car's still at the house,' Kelly pointed out.

'But Missie and Whittaker aren't there, you said?' Dee questioned her.

'Well, I couldn't see or hear them.'

'Hmm… Well, it's all very odd. You don't think she could have gone to Cornwall to see your family, do you?' she asked Beth.

Beth shook her head.

'No, I rang home yesterday and I know that my mother would have said if Anna had been there. I didn't ask her outright because I didn't want to start worrying her; she and Anna have always been close.'

'What are we going to do?' Kelly asked the other two, but it was Dee she was looking at.

Dee pursed her lips.

'If we haven't heard anything by tonight, there's only one thing we can do: we shall have to inform the police.'

'You think it's that serious, then, do you?' Beth faltered. Dee's eyes were bleak.

'Possibly,' was all she would allow herself to say.

Ten minutes later as she drove home, though, she was glad that Beth and Kelly couldn't see into her mind and read her thoughts. She knew that Kelly was curious about why she, Dee, should hate Julian Cox so much, and she knew too that Kelly suspected that there was far more to her hatred of him than just his treatment of Beth.

And she was right.

But it was not Kelly but Anna whom Dee had been increasingly tempted to confide in and talk to about the private demons that drove her. Anna might lack Kelly's vibrant immediate response to things but she possessed her own quiet brand of strength and sometimes Dee yearned to be able to lean on someone else's.

She knew that people found her self-possessed and even a little challenging, but they didn't know what had made her that way, nor why she *had* to be that way.

To confide in anyone, even Anna, would be to risk inflicting terrible damage on someone she had loved very, very dearly and there was no way she could do that, so the burden she had carried on her own for so long was one she would have to go on carrying, and if some people thought her hard and unfeeling, unfeminine, then so be it.

And now, of course, she had another burden to shoulder. If something *had* happened to Anna, how much responsibility did *she* bear for it? *Was* Anna's disappearance connected with the trap they had set for Julian Cox? Had the fifty thousand pounds he had so cleverly snatched from beneath their noses not been enough? Had he come back for more, or perhaps sent someone else? She had promised no harm would come to Kelly and Anna through her plans, so the pressure and guilt were mounting by the minute.

Loath as she was to involve the police—for several reasons—Dee knew she had very little option. Surely Anna's disappearance could have nothing whatsoever to

do with Julian Cox, but that made Dee even more anxious for her safety and not less.

How often had she seen articles in the press about
women—and it was nearly always women—who had
disappeared under mystifying circumstances? In some
cases the body was found later... In some it wasn't.
Dee's knuckles turned white as she gripped the steering
wheel of her car.

'Please God, no,' she whispered. 'No.'

She couldn't go home, she just could not, Anna decided
tiredly as she got off the train and wearily thanked the
porter who helped her with her luggage and her pets.
She felt empty, drained of all emotion. The long train
journey with its numerous changes and stops had given
her plenty of time to think—and remember—and not
just plenty, but too much.

If she went home there would be questions for her to
answer, people for her to see, and she could not bear
it—Ward might even try to get in touch with her, if
only to charge her for the use of his car, she reflected
bitterly.

There was a row of waiting taxis outside the station,
and she hailed one of them.

Once she was settled inside, Missie on her knee,
Whittaker in his carrying cage, the driver turned round
and asked her, 'Where to, love?'

Where to? Good question... Anna closed her eyes
and then, almost as though the words were being spoken
for her, she heard herself giving him Dee's address.

Dee was upstairs lying in the bath, her eyes closed,
her body still and relaxed but her mind furiously busy,
when Anna's taxi arrived. Her bath had, for Dee, always
been a place of safety and retreat, a place to regroup

her energies and marshal her forces. As a teenager, trying to come to terms with so many different emotions
at once, so many physical changes within herself, she
had found the bathroom a place in which she could be
alone without feeling guilty about shutting her father
out. They had always been so close, just the two of them
on their own since her mother's death, but with her
teenage years had come an instinctive female awareness
that now she was moving into the new territory of her
own womanhood.

She had been so protective of her father, sensing his
solitude, his loving absorption in her life. Where, previously, his had been the only company she had wanted,
now she was increasingly experiencing a yearning for
the company of her own age group, for female friends
with whom she could share the mystery and excitement
of what was happening to her. And yet, at the same
time, she had sensed how hurt her father would be by
her alienation from him. Side by side they had battled
it out; her loving daughterly desire to protect him and
her growing need to spread her own wings.

There had been many hours spent in the bathroom
worrying about what she should do: go on to university
as she so longed to do or stay at home with her father.

In the end it had been her father himself who had
resolved her dilemma for her—wiser and more aware
than she had guessed—telling her firmly how disappointed he would be if she did not finish her education
and go to university.

Dee was lost in her thoughts and her memories of
the past when the doorbell rang and, at first, she was
tempted to ignore its summons. Then, reluctantly, she
acknowledged that perhaps she ought to see who it was,

pulling on her robe as she opened the bathroom door and padded quickly downstairs.

'Dee.'

Frowning slightly, Dee peered through the frosted glass of her front door and then, realising just who her visitor was, she quickly unlocked and opened it, exclaiming thankfully, 'Anna! Come in!'

Still semi-dazed with shock, Anna followed Dee into her hallway.

It was a relatively warm day but she had started to shiver, her eyes blank and unfocused as she allowed Dee to take hold of her arm and virtually guide her into the kitchen.

'Sit down,' Dee commanded her firmly, relieving her of Whittaker's cat box and deftly removing Missie's lead from her hand at the same time.

Something very distressing had obviously happened to Anna, Dee recognised as her initial relief at seeing her standing outside her front door was swiftly replaced by concern.

'We've been wondering where you'd got to,' she told Anna chattily as she filled the kettle.

Instinct was warning her not to make too much of a drama of Anna's reappearance, nor to bully her into immediate explanations.

Instead, as she made them both a cup of tea, she kept up a stream of light, inconsequential chatter, telling Anna that she had recently seen both Beth and Kelly, watching her as she did so to see how she reacted, but apart from a brief flicker of her eyelids Anna remained almost motionless. She was not, perhaps, actually catatonic, but she had most certainly undergone some kind of severe trauma, Dee realised, and she, after all, knew all the signs of acute emotional shock.

There were some things you never forgot, some experiences that never faded.

Now, as she put Anna's cup of tea down in front of her, she saw that the other woman was simply staring into space.

'Anna,' she said gently, touching her arm. 'What is it? What's happened? What's wrong?'

What was wrong?

Anna focused despairingly on Dee's face.

'I... I...' Slowly her face crumpled and her body started to shake.

Instinctively Dee put her arms around her, holding her comfortingly.

'If it's about Julian and the money...' she guessed. She knew how distressed Anna had been about the fact that Julian had outwitted them both.

'No. No...' Anna shook her head and then stopped.

'Then what is it? What's wrong?' Dee asked her gently.

Anna put a trembling hand up to her face. She still wasn't sure what she was doing here in Dee's kitchen or really why she had come. All she did know was that she simply could not go back to her own house.

'Dee, I've been such a fool,' Anna told her dully. Tears welled up in her eyes. 'I should have known, guessed, but instead...' She gripped her hands into angry fists, her body shuddering in self-loathing. 'I don't know what came over me...or why...'

Patiently Dee waited, listening to her incoherent utterances for several minutes before coaxing, 'Anna, why don't you start at the beginning and tell me everything?'

'Everything...?' Anna's face changed colour, going pink and then white. 'I can't...tell you everything,' she said flatly. 'Some of it.' She paused and shook her head.

'Oh, Dee, I just don't know what I'm going to do, how I'm going to get over…'

How I'm going to get over Ward, she had been about to say, Anna recognised, but she had managed to stop herself. How many times did she have to remind herself that the Ward she had believed she loved simply did not exist? In reality, there was no Ward, no lover for her to get over.

'Tell me,' Dee repeated softly.

Slowly, haltingly at first, Anna started to explain what had happened.

'He did what?' Dee demanded flatly in disbelief when Anna explained about the mistake at the hospital and how she had assumed that Ward was her lover.

'He…this man, this stranger, who less than twelve hours previously had been threatening you…actually allowed you to believe that you and he were lovers…?'

The furious outrage in Dee's voice made Anna bite her bottom lip.

'I've been thinking about it over and over again,' she told Dee in a low voice. '*I* was the one who assumed that we were lovers. *I'm* to blame for that and—'

'You were suffering from amnesia,' Dee reminded her grimly.

'He knew perfectly well what the real relationship— if it can be called a relationship—was between you. He should never…' She stopped, her eyes flashing with contempt. 'Of all the underhanded, conniving…'

'I thought he loved me,' Anna told her shakily, 'but all the time he actually *hated* me, loathed me…'

Closing her eyes, she placed her hand over her mouth to silence the sobs of emotion she could feel rising in her throat.

'I never suspected anything; I truly believed…'

Dee watched her silently. She didn't want to upset Anna by questioning just how far the deception had gone. It appalled her to know that Anna had been victimised, and in such a cruel and dangerous way, and she could well understand why her friend felt that she didn't want to return to her own home where she would be on her own.

'What I don't understand is how on earth anyone could possibly justify such behaviour,' Dee breathed furiously when Anna had eventually told her everything. 'What possible motivation could he have had?'

'He wanted his half-brother's money back,' Anna told her quietly.

She was beginning to feel slightly more in control now. Telling Dee what had happened, painful though it had been, had had a cathartic effect on her, helping to ground her a little better and make her feel more like her normal self instead of as though some unfamiliar stranger was inhabiting her body and her emotions.

'He did *that* to you for money?' Dee demanded savagely.

'No, not just for *money*,' Anna told her, shaking her head. 'I think there must have been a certain degree of revenge and punishment in it for him…'

'What? How could *anyone*…?' Dee began, but Anna shook her head, giving Dee a small, painful smile.

'*We* did,' she reminded her dryly. 'Or at least we tried to with Julian…'

'Oh, yes, but that wasn't the same thing at all,' Dee protested quickly. 'There's no way anyone could compare *you* with Julian. You weren't in any way responsible for Julian's scams…'

'You and I might know that, but Ward…' She

paused, and had to swallow hard before she was able to continue speaking. 'Ward thought I was.'

'But to deceive you like that. To...'

'To pretend that he loved me? Take me to bed?' Anna gave a brief mirthless laugh. 'He did actually try to insist that we had separate rooms. I was the one who...' She stopped again.

'Oh, Dee,' she wept. 'I feel so...so degraded, so...so—' She broke off. There were some things that were just too painful to discuss.

'Well, at least you're back and you're safe; that's the main thing,' Dee told her briskly. When she saw Anna's face she touched her arm a little awkwardly and told her gruffly, 'I know you won't think it possible right now, but eventually time will soften... You'll feel...it won't seem so bad as it does right now. After all, you're over the worst, you've experienced that already, so, logically, things can only get better.'

Anna gave her a small wry smile.

'What did he say when you confronted him, when you told him that you knew the truth?' Dee asked her. 'Did he express any kind of remorse, try to make any kind of explanation or apology...?'

'No...' Anna began, and then, when she saw Dee's outraged expression, she told her shakily, 'I didn't confront him. I...I just left him a note saying that I'd remembered everything; that I knew... I couldn't bear... I just wanted to get away, Dee,' she told her. 'You see...' She paused and a single tear rolled betrayingly down her pale face. 'You see...' Despairingly she twisted the damp tissue she was holding in her fingers. 'I really thought I loved him; I really believed... He seemed so...so right,' she told Dee helplessly. 'Being with him felt so right... It was as though...it was as

though he filled in all the missing pieces of my life, as
though he completed it and me in a way that I'd never
dreamed I could *be* complete. It was as though he…
Even now I can't really believe… It all seems like a
dream…'

'Nightmare, more like,' Dee told her angrily as she
leaned over to take her in a protective hug.

Anna smiled sadly. It was crazy, humiliating and dangerous, she knew, but deep down inside she knew that
a part of her was always going to ache and long for
him, that that part of her which he had touched so vi-
brantly and brought to life so immediately and intensely
was always going to yearn for him. No amount of righ-
teous anger, of bitterness and contempt, or logical emotional response to what he had done, was ever going to
completely wipe out of her memory the sweetness of
what they had shared, even though she now knew it had
been a poison-tipped sweetness.

But that was her secret, her cross to bear for the rest
of her life.

'I'd love to have him here right now to give him a
piece of my mind,' Dee told her with angry contempt.
'To do something like that, to you of all people…'

She saw that Anna's eyes were filling with tears
again.

'Come on,' she told her gently. 'Let's get you upstairs and in bed. You look exhausted.'

'No. I'm fine,' Anna protested, but she still obediently followed Dee towards the stairs.

'So how is Anna now?' Kelly asked Dee anxiously.
'What did the doctor say? Is she…?'

'She's fine,' Dee assured the other girl, tucking the
telephone receiver under her chin so that she could

stroke Missie, who was as anxious about Anna as the
rest of them were. 'The doctor has given her the all-
clear medically; he said, though, that she needed to rest
as she's obviously undergone a tremendous amount of
trauma.'

At Anna's specific request, Dee had kept the details
of Ward's role in what had happened to her to an ab-
solute minimum. So far as Kelly and Beth knew, Ward
was simply someone who had stepped in to help her
after her accident and subsequent loss of memory—a
good Samaritan, so to speak, even though it had practically choked Dee to have to refer to him as such.

'Did she say why she went away—or where?' Kelly
asked Dee curiously.

'Oh, she just felt like a few days away,' Dee responded airily and, she hoped, dismissively enough not
to further arouse Kelly's curiosity, but despite her outwardly relaxed manner inwardly Dee was seething with
fury over the way Ward Hunter had behaved towards
her friend. How could he possibly have thought she was
the kind of woman who would get involved in anything
even vaguely underhand? Anna was the type of woman
who panicked if she couldn't get a parking ticket out
of the machine and instead left a message plus an IOU
for the car park attendant—and, even if he had thought
she was involved in some kind of criminal activity with
Julian Cox, to have done to her what he had done...

Dee closed her eyes as she replaced her telephone
receiver after Kelly's call. Why, why were they the way
they were? For every man like her own father and
Kelly's Brough there were ten—no, a hundred—who
seemed to deliberately go out of their way to hurt the
woman they professed to love. Dee carried her own

scars from the war she believed existed between the sexes, but that was another story.

A little ruefully Dee admitted that she had perhaps been rather heavy-handed, in more than one sense, with the large brandy she had insisted on Anna drinking earlier in the evening, but it had had the desired effect and now Anna was getting some much needed sleep. The trauma of her temporary amnesia was something that anyone would find difficult to come to terms with, never mind the added misery and anguish Anna had been caused, Dee reflected as she checked that Anna's pets were secure in their new temporary home.

She still had some financial reports to read before she went to bed. The responsibility of handling her father's complex financial empire was one she took extremely seriously. His death had been totally unexpected, and it had thrown her head-first into relatively unfamiliar work, but Dee had felt she owed it to him to become familiar with it and to ensure that his business interests generated enough money to service his varied philanthropic activities.

The only changes she had made were such that his financial generosity to the various charities he had helped had been made public, so that other people would know, as she had known, just what a very special and caring man her father had been.

There were times when she still missed him very badly. If he could see her now, would he be disappointed in her? she wondered. He had been a little old-fashioned in some ways, and she knew he would have wanted her to marry and have children. But how could she do that? There was enough of him in her for her to know that she could only make that kind of commitment to someone if she truly loved them and was loved by them in return. And how could that ever be possible when she didn't believe that love, the kind of love she had dreamed of as a young girl, actually existed? Love was simply a word used to cloak far more practical and less ideological emotions. Love, or rather the promise of it, was just a weapon men used against women.

'I love you,' they said, but what they meant was, 'I love myself.'

'You'd better watch it,' she mocked Whittaker playfully. 'There aren't many males brave enough to come into this house!'

CHAPTER ELEVEN

'How is he?'

Ward put down the article he had been reading as his mother came out of his stepfather's hospital room, closing the door behind her.

Instantly his mother's face broke into a relaxed smile.

'He's feeling much better. The specialist just wants to have a few words with him and then he... He saw the specialist this morning and he's confirmed that it wasn't a heart attack after all. They've got all the test results back now and he thinks the pain was caused by anxiety.

'You know how your stepfather is, and he's been worrying about this trip Ritchie is planning to make to America...'

Ward made a small, explosive sound before getting up and reassuring his mother.

'There's no need for him to worry about *anything*...'

'I know that, dear, but you know what he's like. He feels it isn't fair that you're having to finance Ritchie through university when you...'

She stopped and Ward gave her a wry look.

'When I what? When I had to work my own way through life? Ma, for heaven's sake, surely he doesn't think I begrudge Ritchie the chance—'

'No. No, of course he doesn't,' his mother reassured him quickly. 'He knows how fond you are of Ritchie, Ward,' she told her elder son, placing her hand on his arm. 'We both do. You've done so much for all of us.

I just wish…You really ought to marry again, you know,' she told him gently. 'Have children… I know that…' She stopped and then looked at him intently.

'You've met someone, haven't you? Don't deny it, Ward. I can see it in your eyes…'

Ward was too taken aback to deny her maternal perception, stating curtly, 'I don't want to talk about it, and anyway—' He broke off, his mouth hardening.

Perhaps it wasn't really surprising that his mother had guessed about Anna. After all, he had barely stopped thinking about her from the moment he had read her note. Even in his most anxious moments for his stepfather, Anna had still been there in his thoughts, tormenting him, haunting him.

He had tried telling himself that everything he had done had been justified; that he had owed it to Ritchie and her other victims to do what he had done, but, instead of being able to focus on her crime, all he had really been able to do was remember how she had felt in his arms, how she had smelled, tasted, *been*, and how much he was missing her, how damnably much.

'Tell me about her,' his mother insisted with firm maternal authority.

Ward glanced towards his stepfather's closed hospital-room door, but it was obvious that no help or rescue was going to come from that area.

'There isn't anything *to* tell,' he informed his mother brusquely. 'Oh, you needn't look at me like that.' He gave a bitter laugh. 'It's not what you're thinking; it's no match made in heaven, Ma, far more like one made in hell.'

His skin darkened slightly as he saw the look of mingled despair and compassion in his mother's eyes.

'She's a liar and the next damned thing to being a

thief,' he told her baldly. 'By rights there's no way I should feel about her the way I do, but...' He stopped and shook his head. 'And, even if she felt the same way about me, which now that she knows...' He stopped again.

'Tell me,' his mother repeated.

'You won't like it,' he warned her grimly.

Twenty minutes later, when he had finished, his mother's face was pale.

'You're right,' she told him in a strained voice. 'I *don't* like it. Oh, Ward,' she burst out painfully. 'How *could* you do such a thing? That poor girl. What *must* she have felt?'

'That poor girl?' Ward exploded. 'Ma, she's the one—' He stopped, pushing his fingers into his hair. 'If anyone needs your sympathy then...'

'Ward, she must have been so hurt and shocked. To have believed you loved her as much as she obviously loves you...'

'Hang on a minute... What makes you think she loves me?' Ward demanded sharply.

'But it's so obvious,' his mother replied gently. 'If she didn't love you she would never have... Ward, of *course* she loves you,' she told him severely.

'Ma, you're behaving as though...' He hesitated and shook his head in frustration. 'I told you. The reason I went to see her in the first place was because...'

'Because she cheated Ritchie out of five thousand pounds,' his mother agreed serenely. 'Yes, I know. But, Ward, have you thought she could have had a reason for her behaviour? There could have been mitigating circumstances...'

'For what's damn near fraud?' Ward demanded scornfully. 'Ma...'

'Is it really so important what she did, Ward?' his mother asked him quietly. 'You've as good as said yourself that you love her. I know that she must love you.'

'Of course it's important,' Ward told her harshly. 'If a person is inherently dishonest, how can you have a trusting relationship with them? How could I ever...?'

'Ward, I've never told you this, but when I first knew your stepfather there'd been a spate of thefts from the school—only small amounts of money were involved, but they were thefts nonetheless. *I* knew and so did your stepfather that all the circumstantial evidence pointed to me being the thief. Your stepfather had every reason to believe that I *was* a thief, but he still put his feelings for me and the fact that he had fallen in love with me above all the logical facts that indicated that I was responsible for taking money from the school.'

'But you weren't the thief,' Ward pointed out grimly, 'and Anna...'

'Ward, you aren't listening to me,' his mother told him gently. 'Just as you aren't listening to your heart. You should do. Sometimes it gives a much truer message than one's brain.

'Go and see her,' she counselled him. 'Go and see your Anna, Ward, and tell her what you've told me. Tell her that you love her.'

He wasn't going to, of course. What was the point? He had already made a complete fool of himself over her once, telling her that he loved her, but fate had intervened, giving him a second chance to get his life back under his own control, giving him a second chance to listen to the logical, analytical messages of his brain rather than the emotional ones of his heart.

No, he wasn't going to pay any attention whatsoever

to what his mother had said, to what he himself was feeling…

So why, just as soon as he had assured himself that his stepfather was on the mend, was he driving far too fast along a motorway which would not take him home to Yorkshire but instead to Rye?

Because his mother was right, that was why. Because he loved Anna and he couldn't let her go without at least seeing her one more time.

One more time. Just who was he kidding? Ward asked himself with grim black humour.

He loved Anna, and he loved her so deeply and so intensely that… That what? That he was prepared to abandon his principles and his beliefs for her? That he thought he could totally suspend reality and pretend that she had not done what they both knew she had done?

And what of Anna herself? What if she did not *want* to change? What if she enjoyed cheating and deceiving? What if he took her his offer of amnesty and a completely new beginning and she threw it back in his face?

But somehow Ward could not imagine the Anna he had come to know and love so intimately ever behaving like that. She had shown such tenderness and compassion, such concerned awareness for the feelings of others, that it would, quite simply, be totally out of character for her to do that kind of thing.

But had he actually known the real Anna? Perhaps her blow on the head had affected *more* than just her memory. What was he trying to persuade himself to believe? Ward asked himself scornfully. That Anna had undergone a complete personality change? Now he was venturing into the realms of fantasy.

But still, when the opportunity came half an hour

later for him to switch motorways and drive straight
home, he made no attempt to take it.

'Are you sure you really feel well enough to be home?'
Dee asked Anna sternly as they stood in Anna's kitchen.

'Dee, I'm fine,' Anna responded gently.

Dee had tried every argument she could think of to
persuade Anna to change her mind and stay on as her
guest instead of going back to her own house, but Anna
had remained obdurate and Dee had finally been persuaded to drive her home.

'I have to get my life back to normal some time,' she
had responded with a brisk lack of self pity when Dee
had suggested that perhaps she needed more time to
come to terms with what had happened, before returning
home where she would be on her own.

'I think it is much better that I should get back into
the swing of things sooner rather than later,' Anna insisted now. 'Not that I don't appreciate all that you've
done for me,' she told Dee warmly. 'Without you...'
She stopped and shook her head. 'It's made me feel so
much better just having someone to talk things over
with, and I'm grateful to you as well, Dee, for keeping
what I've told you between the two of us. It's bad
enough that I've made such a complete fool of myself
anyway...'

'I'm sure that Kelly and Beth would have understood,' Dee told her quickly and truthfully.

'Yes. I know they would, but... Beth seems to be
over Julian but she's changed...she's different. There's
something on her mind, something that's worrying her,
but whatever it is she just doesn't seem to want to talk
about it.'

'Mmm... I must admit I *have* noticed that she does

seem to be rather preoccupied lately,' Dee agreed, 'but I'd put that down to the problems she seems to be having with this stuff she ordered when she was in Prague.'

'Oh, dear, has she still not received that order?' Anna asked her. 'Poor Beth; I hope it arrives soon. I know she was counting on it to boost her sales.'

'Mmm... Well, she's got time yet,' Dee reminded her.

'You've been such a wonderful friend to all of us, Dee,' Anna praised her. 'You've helped us all and—'

'Helped you?' Dee interrupted her dryly. 'Have I? *I* was responsible for nearly turning Kelly and Brough against one another, and now it's because I involved you in lending Julian money that this Ward Hunter has behaved so badly towards you...'

Anna looked quickly at Dee. There were still times when she tended to forget that Dee was actually younger than her, times when all of them tended to lean on her, but Anna recognised that Dee too had her moments of insecurity, her moments of vulnerability.

'You are a good friend,' she reiterated softly now. 'A very good friend, Dee. I just wish...' She stopped and looked searchingly at her. 'I don't want to pry but...this thing between you and Julian Cox. There's more to it than you've ever told any of us, I think...'

Anna waited, holding her breath, wondering if Dee would take the opportunity she was trying to give her to confide in her as Anna had done in her, and, for a moment, she thought her patience was going to be rewarded as Dee began hesitantly, 'Yes, there is, and...'

'And...?' Anna encouraged.

Dee looked away from her.

'I can't... It isn't anything really,' she told her dismissively, and Anna knew that there was no point in trying to press her any further. She knew something else as well, she acknowledged a little sadly as Dee announced that she would go out to the car to bring in the rest of Anna's things, and the shopping they had just bought. She knew that Dee was lying to her.

She couldn't make Dee confide in her, but what she could do, Anna decided as she gave in to Dee's insistence and agreed that, yes, perhaps she would go upstairs and rest on her bed for a while, was to make sure that if Dee did ever need her—for any reason—she was there for her.

'Look, I've got to go and do some supermarket shopping,' Dee told her. 'If there's anything that you want I could get it for you and we could perhaps have lunch here together…'

Anna hesitated before accepting Dee's offer. She was perfectly well enough to go and do her own supermarket shopping now that she was home, but if she was honest she knew that if anyone were to ask her the kind of questions she could not bring herself to answer… It was still too soon, her emotions still too raw.

'I shan't be long,' Dee assured her, heading for the door.

The last thing she felt like doing was sleeping, Anna admitted after Dee had gone, but nevertheless she lay down on the bed and closed her eyes, opening them quickly a few minutes later as the telephone beside the bed rang. Reaching for the receiver, she said, 'Hello?'

'Hello,' she heard a woman's voice responding warmly. 'Am I speaking to Anna Trewayne?'

'Yes, you are,' Anna confirmed. 'But who—?'

'My name is Ruth. I'm Ward's mother…'

Ward's *mother*! Anna nearly dropped the receiver; her heart was thudding frantically, her immediate instinct being to replace the receiver and blot out the woman's soft, warm voice. But as though she had guessed what Anna was thinking Ruth begged her, 'Please listen to me, Anna. Please…'

Dazed, Anna did as she had requested.

Ward's mother, as Anna soon discovered, had a very good understanding of her son, his bad points as well as his good ones.

'I'm not trying to make excuses for him, and certainly do not intend to make his apologies for him,' she told Anna firmly. 'But what I do want to say, Anna, is that he loves you very much.'

'He didn't love me at the hospital when he allowed me to believe that we were lovers,' Anna countered quietly.

'No,' his mother agreed immediately. 'He didn't love you then, but, after all, he didn't know you then.'

'He deliberately and callously took advantage of my vulnerability,' Anna pointed out remorselessly.

'Yes,' his mother conceded, without attempting to defend him. 'And the fact that he believed you had done the same thing to Ritchie in no way excuses that behaviour,' she added firmly.

On her end of the line Anna smiled rather ruefully at that quick and very sure maternal thrust.

'Why are you telling me all of this?' she asked Ward's mother eventually.

'Because I'm a woman as well as a mother,' she came back immediately. 'And I know that as a woman you need to know that your own instincts and feelings didn't betray you. That what you and Ward shared *was* real and that he *does* love you.'

'I love you,' he had told her after making love with her, and in the bitterness of discovering how he had deceived her Anna had considered those words to be as much a fiction as everything else he had told her. But what if they had not been? What if they had been the truth—still were the truth?

'Has he asked you to tell me all of this?' Anna asked her challengingly.

'No. Ward's a very proud and independent man. He won't like what I've done at all.'

'So why have you done it?' Anna asked her.

There was a brief pause before his mother, sounding heart-rendingly like a female version of Ward, told her seriously, 'Because I wanted to know myself what the woman my proud and picky elder son has fallen so completely in love with is like.'

'And you can tell that from a phone call?' Anna derided gently.

'*You* could tell *you* loved him through your amnesia,' his mother retorted, before adding wisely, 'Our sex have very well-attuned emotional instincts.'

'And what you're saying is that because I love him I should just ignore what he's done, the way he's behaved…'

'Certainly not,' Ward's mother returned with a touch of asperity. 'All I wanted to do, Anna, is to tell you plainly and simply that Ward loves you. I'm his mother; my natural instinct is to help and protect him—despite the fact that at forty-two he's more than adult enough to take charge of his own life and to make his own decisions.'

'And if I hadn't told you that Ward got it wrong, that I had absolutely nothing whatsoever to do with Julian Cox's shabby schemes, that I was as much a victim of him as your Ritchie, then how would you have felt?'

'No different,' Ward's mother told her promptly and,

Anna could tell, truthfully. 'And to tell you the truth it pleases me more than you can imagine that Ward has been forced to admit that he loves you even though he thinks that you *are* in cahoots with Julian Cox. I'd begun to despair of him ever letting down his guard with anyone, or ever allowing himself to listen to his emotions. Had he produced some perfect woman he had chosen to become involved with because he thought she would make him a good wife, I would have been very upset. Ward needed to be shown that he's only human, that his emotions cannot be controlled or contained. The fact that he thinks so badly of you and yet still loves you so much...' She paused and then laughed before adding wryly, 'Of course, I don't pretend not to be very, very pleased to hear that my darling and oh, so idiotic son has got it so very, very wrong... I can't wait to meet you for myself, Anna...'

Then it was Anna's turn to laugh.

'Don't count your chickens,' she warned her a little shakily. 'Ward may have told *you* that he loves me and that my supposedly nefarious behaviour hasn't destroyed that love, but that doesn't necessarily mean he's going to do anything about it, nor that I would want him to,' Anna felt bound to point out a little hardily.

'Oh, but he will,' his mother told Anna very positively, pausing again before admitting, 'I don't believe in interfering in my sons' lives—at least not normally—but during our...er...discussion it struck me that in the heat of the moment Ward might have been, shall we say, a little irresponsible—neglectful of the consequences of what he was doing...'

It took several seconds for what she was saying to sink into Anna's consciousness fully, but once it had she sat bolt upright on her bed, her face flushing a hot

pink with the recognition that Ward wasn't the only one
who had perhaps behaved irresponsibly.

'Oh, but that's…' 'Impossible,' she had been about
to say, but of course it wasn't, and what was more…
Anna took a deep breath. Suddenly her bedroom seemed
to be filled with sunshine. Suddenly she felt absolutely
on top of the world; suddenly that world had become a
wonderfully exciting place.

A baby… Why on earth hadn't she…?

'There's just no way Ward would ever turn his back
on his child or its mother,' Ward's mother told Anna
quietly. 'But there is one point I should make, I think,
Anna. When you do tell Ward the truth about your relationship with Julian Cox, don't be surprised if he isn't
as pleased and relieved to hear it as you expect. He *will*
be pleased, of course, but he's also going to feel very
much at a disadvantage with you because of it, and very
ashamed of his own misjudgement of you. It will be
one thing for Ward to offer you the generosity of his
understanding of your errors, but he will find it very
hard to accept your generosity over his.'

'Yes,' Anna agreed simply, knowing what Ward's
mother had told her was perfectly true.

When she replaced the receiver she felt so elated and
excited that she could barely contain her emotions. She
wanted to get up, get dressed, sing, shout, laugh. Ward
loved her… Ward had never meant to humiliate or deceive her; he had simply seized the moment, just as she
had seized him!

A baby…

Anna made a soft crooning sound of pleasure beneath
her breath.

Dee was just about to turn into Anna's drive when she
saw the large Mercedes behind her, signalling to do the

same. Frowning, she stopped her own car and got out. She knew that Anna wasn't expecting any visitors. Warily she approached the now motionless Mercedes.

Its driver was instantly recognisable to her from Anna's description.

'Where do you think you're going?' she demanded angrily.

Ward stared at her. Who on earth was this virago?

'I was actually intending to visit Anna—not that it's any of your business,' he returned coolly.

The young woman standing in front of him was quite plainly on the warpath but Ward had no idea why she should be—nor did he wish to find out. All he wanted to do was to see Anna, to hold her in his arms, to tell her how much he loved her...

Dee stared at him. She could scarcely believe the man's effrontery.

'Don't you think you've already done enough, *hurt* her enough?' she demanded furiously. 'I know exactly who you are *and* what you've done, and if you think for one minute that Anna could want to see you...'

Ward frowned.

'She's discussed me with you?'

'She's told me *everything*,' Dee informed him acidly.

Ward's frown deepened. This very angry young woman standing in his way wasn't a complication he had expected.

'Where *is* Anna?' he asked Dee curtly, looking past her towards the house.

'She isn't here,' Dee fibbed. 'She's gone away. And even if she was here,' she told Ward fiercely, 'there's no way she would want to see you after the way you've lied to her, deceived her...'

'Just a minute,' Ward objected grimly. 'I had my reasons for doing what I did.'

'If by "reasons" you mean your erroneous belief that Anna was involved in one of Julian Cox's scams, then I have to tell you that you got it completely wrong,' Dee told him scornfully. 'Anna was as much a victim of his deceit as your brother.'

Ward stared at her.

'I don't know what you're trying to say, but I know for a fact that Anna and Julian Cox were partners.'

'Don't you mean you know for a fact that you saw a piece of paper *claiming* that they were partners?' Dee queried fiercely. 'It's a pity you didn't check your facts a little more carefully. Had you done so you might have discovered the truth.'

'What truth?'

'The truth that Julian Cox simply used Anna's name without either her knowledge or her permission.'

'If that's true then why didn't Anna tell me that herself?' Ward questioned Dee.

'Perhaps she would have done so had she been given the chance and had she not been suffering from amnesia,' Dee told him frostily.

Ward studied Dee's set face. There was no doubt that she was speaking the truth.

'If *you* had been honest with Anna, if you'd told her at the hospital just who you were and why you were there, no doubt in time, when she had regained her memory, she could have told you just how wrong you were in assuming that she was Julian's partner.'

Ward paused for a moment before retaliating hotly, 'If that's the truth, then why didn't she tell me when she had the opportunity the first time we met?'

Now it was Dee's turn to pause.

'She didn't tell you because she wanted to speak with me first,' she told him reluctantly.

'To speak with you?'

'Yes,' Dee confirmed.

It was obvious to her that Ward was waiting for a more detailed explanation, but why should she give him one? After what he had done to Anna he didn't deserve an explanation—he didn't deserve anything.

'Have you *any* idea just what you've done to Anna, just how much you've hurt her? You let her think...' Dee stopped, pressing her lips together. 'Do you really think there's any way she'd want to see or speak with you ever again? You've had your pound of flesh and your money.'

'Is that her decision or yours?' Ward demanded bitingly, but Dee refused to be intimidated.

'Anna's my friend and it's my right as her friend to protect her. I blame myself in part for what you've done to her. The only reason she ever got involved with Julian Cox in the first place was to help me.'

'To help you? Why? What is Cox to you? An ex-lover...?'

'No,' Dee denied sharply.

'You're accusing *me* of behaving unfairly towards Anna, but it seems to me that you've scarcely treated her very kindly yourself,' Ward accused Dee angrily. 'By exposing her to Cox's malice and—'

'*I* didn't tell Anna that I loved her. *I* didn't allow her to believe we were lovers. *I* didn't take her to bed and—' Abruptly Dee stopped, suddenly conscious that she had said too much, trespassed too far into private and intimate territory.

It was useless trying to talk to this aggressive and angry young woman, Ward decided, and if he continued to stand here and argue with her he was going to be in danger of losing his own temper. He was still trying to come to terms with the bombshell Dee had dropped with her revelations regarding the truth about Anna's relationship with Julian Cox.

Strangely, despite his resentment at the way Dee was speaking to him, Ward knew instinctively that what she was telling him *was* the truth. Suddenly everything clicked into place. No wonder he had been so confused about the apparent dichotomy in his misjudgement of Anna's character and the way he had seen her behave. It made him feel as if someone was twisting a knife in his heart to know how badly he had misjudged Anna, how despicably he had treated her. No wonder she didn't want to see or hear from him again. He couldn't blame her.

It had been one thing to tell himself that his love for her was so strong that he could overlook her involvement with Julian Cox, it was quite another to have to acknowledge how totally their roles had just been reversed.

And, besides, even if Anna allowed him to talk to her for long enough for him to tell her that he had known how much he loved her *before* he had discovered the truth about her, Ward was afraid that he simply wouldn't be able to convince her. After all, in her shoes, he would not have been easy to convince.

He had treated her in the most cruel and unjustifiable way and it served him right that she now no longer wanted anything to do with him.

Without another word he turned round and walked back to his car.

Dee watched him get in and drive away before climbing back into her own car and driving up to Anna's house.

'Anna, what are you doing out of bed?' she asked as she opened the kitchen door and found Anna humming as she filled the kettle.

'I feel so much better that I didn't want to stay in bed any longer. After all, I'm not an invalid, you know,' Anna responded dryly. '*You* don't look very happy,' she added perceptively. 'Something's wrong. What is it?'

Dee, who had had no intention of telling Anna anything whatsoever about her run-in with Ward, suddenly discovered to her own chagrin that she was actually flushing a little as she tried to mumble a protective fib.

'Oh, it's no good,' she finally admitted. 'I shall have to tell you. Anna, just... I was just turning into your drive when...when Ward Hunter turned in after me.'

'Ward's here? Where?' Anna demanded, immediately flying to the kitchen window to peer out into the garden.

'No, he's not here,' Dee told her. 'I...I told him that you wouldn't want to see him and, in fact, I actually told him that you weren't even here.'

'He's gone? When? Just now? Oh, heavens, that means... Dee, I have to go after him. He'll have gone home; I know the way.'

'Go after him? What? After what he's done...?' Dee looked stunned.

'No, it isn't like you think,' Anna assured her, quickly explaining to Dee what Ward's mother had told her during their telephone call.

'And you believe her, do you?' Dee asked Anna.

'Yes, I do,' Anna confirmed quietly.

Dee was both startled and impressed by Anna's unfamiliar decisiveness and determination.

'It seems I've done the wrong thing, then, in sending him away,' she commented ruefully. 'I'm sorry, Anna, but I…'

'It's not your fault. After all, you didn't know about Ward's mother's phone call. I know you just wanted to protect me, Dee, and I'm truly grateful to you for that,' Anna told her friend, hugging her. 'Can I ask you a favour, by the way?' When Dee nodded Anna asked her, 'Could you look after Missie and Whittaker for me? I don't know when I shall be back—later this evening, if Ward refuses to listen to me.'

'Yes, I'll look after them,' Dee agreed. 'It's the least I can do.'

CHAPTER TWELVE

WARD hadn't eaten anything since breakfast but as he forced himself to go through the motions of preparing a meal he acknowledged that he didn't really have any appetite for it.

What was Anna doing now? Where was she? He only hoped that wherever she was she was being treated with tenderness and the love she so much deserved, the tenderness and love *he* should have given her, he should *be* giving her, he *so* longed to give her.

As he had driven north he had kept picturing her in the hospital when she had looked up at him, her eyes shining with relief and love; at her house when she had turned her head and smiled at him; in his bed when she had told him, shown him...

Ward could almost taste the bitterness of his own pain. His eyes felt gritty and sore. He pulled open the fridge door and then closed it again, blinking fiercely. He had switched on the radio when he had come in, hoping that the sound would blot out the agony of his thoughts, but the voice of the woman talking jarred on him. The only voice he longed to hear was Anna's quiet, soft one, the one she used after they had made love, all warm and tender with the emotion of what they had shared.

'Oh, God, Anna!'

'Yes, Ward?'

He swung round in disbelief, opening his eyes, which

he had closed as he had cried out her name in helpless longing and despair.

'Anna... What are you doing here...?'

Anna smiled tremulously at him.

It had been such a relief to drive into the courtyard and discover that his car was here, but now the courage and determination which had brought her in hot pursuit of him had been overwhelmed by her awareness of the risk she was taking, the way she was exposing herself to further hurt and rejection. Only Ward wasn't looking at her as though he was going to reject her. He was looking at her as though...

Anna took a tentative step towards him and then stopped as he abruptly turned his back on her and re-opened the fridge door.

There was so much they both needed to say, so many potential dangers and hazards in doing so that she was afraid they might still lose one another in a morass of explanations and apologies.

There had to be a way she could reach out to him, tell him...show him...

And suddenly, as she studied his back, remembering achingly how it had felt beneath her fingertips, the skin so smooth and taut over his muscles, the breadth of his shoulders so thrillingly masculine and powerful, she knew what it was.

Taking a deep breath, she asked him gently, 'You might want to turn your back on me, Ward, but do you want to turn your back on your son or daughter as well?'

The speed with which he moved surprised her. One minute he was opening the fridge, the next he was jerking her forward against his body into his arms, demanding thickly, 'What are you saying, Anna? My God, woman, are you really...? Have we...?'

Behind her back Anna crossed her fingers, hoping that Mother Nature wasn't going to make a liar out of her as she told him shakily, 'It's early days yet, but yes, Ward, I...I think we have...'

'A child—you're having my child...'

'Our child,' Anna corrected him firmly.

Ward shook his head, groaning.

'My mother warned me that this could have happened, but I thought she was exaggerating the risk...'

'I think maybe we were the ones who did that,' Anna told him demurely.

'You're pregnant...with my child...' Ward repeated. He was running his hands tenderly over her body, his eyes dark with emotion. Anna could feel his fingers trembling slightly as he cupped her face.

'Oh, God, Anna, I've missed you so much,' he told her rawly, adding, 'Can you ever forgive me?'

He was a very proud man and Anna knew how much it must be costing him to ask for her forgiveness and understanding. Another woman might have been tempted to punish him a little more, to remind him of just what he had done and how much he had hurt her, but Anna's gentle nature did not incline her that way.

'We both made mistakes and got things wrong,' she told him softly, adding truthfully, 'We've been very lucky, Ward, because we've been given the chance to start again.'

'I loved you before your friend told me the truth about Cox,' Ward told her huskily.

'I know; you told me so—after we made love...'

'You heard that? I...' He smiled painfully.

'I heard it,' Anna confirmed. 'And even if I hadn't,'

she added in a more light-hearted voice, 'I would have to believe that you love me because your mother told me so.'

'My mother? She's spoken to you? But…'

'But what?' Anna demanded provocatively, lifting her mouth towards his.

'But nothing,' Ward responded thickly, accepting the soft invitation of her half-parted lips with the hungry pressure of his own. 'Hell, Anna, you shouldn't be allowing me to do this,' he groaned as he kissed her. 'There are things we ought to talk about, explanations I ought to make; apologies…I need…

'What is it?' he demanded as she tried to silence him by placing her fingertips against his mouth.

'Later,' Anna told him simply. 'Take me to bed, Ward. I want that so much. I want *you* so much,' she breathed ecstatically as he started to kiss gently and then nibble the fingers she had touched to his lips.

'If we go to bed now, I'm not sure I dare trust myself,' Ward confessed as he held Anna's face and looked deep into her eyes.

'*I* trust you,' Anna told him steadily—and meant it.

'Oh, Anna…'

Anna could see the emotion in his eyes darkening their colour and sparkling on his lashes.

'We both…misinterpreted the facts,' Anna told him gently. 'But, Ward, if *you* hadn't thought I was Julian's partner and if *I* hadn't thought we were lovers, then we would never have had…this…'

'How could I ever, ever have misjudged you so badly?' Ward groaned as he reached for her.

'Ward…? I've been thinking,' Anna murmured happily over an hour later as she lay nestled at Ward's side in bed.

'Hmm…' he responded. 'I don't want to think; I just want to hold you and touch you, kiss you and—'

'Ward,' Anna protested half-heartedly, snuggling blissfully and murmuring her appreciation of the way he was lovingly nibbling at the delicate flesh of her throat. However, as his hand reached out to cup her breast, she caught hold of it and told him severely, 'It's about the baby…'

Immediately she had his attention.

'I'd like Dee to be his or her godmother,' Anna told him quietly.

'Dee?' Ward demanded suspiciously, knowing the answer to his question even before he had asked it. 'She wouldn't be that man-hating virago who refused to allow me to see you this afternoon, would she?'

Anna shook her head chidingly.

'Dee isn't a man-hater, Ward, and as for her being a virago… Underneath she's really very kind—and I think very vulnerable. I promise you, once you get to know her you'll like her,' Anna coaxed him lovingly.

'I'll try to believe you,' Ward offered ruefully. 'But right now,' he added in a softer voice, 'I've got far more important things on my mind…'

'Oh? What things?' Anna teased him.

'Come here and let me show you,' Ward said tenderly.

THE telephone was ringing as Beth hurried back into the shop. She had just nipped out to buy some sandwiches for her own and Kelly's lunch and Kelly was reaching for the receiver as Beth walked in.

'It's for you,' she told Beth, holding out the receiver. 'Someone from Customs and Excise about that stuff you ordered from the Czech Republic.'

Handing Kelly the sandwiches, Beth hurried to pick up the phone, relief washing over her. She had begun to think that her order would never arrive. She had begun to think, she admitted to herself, that Alex might just have been right after all when he had warned her against buying the pretty reproduction antique glassware she had fallen in love with.

'I'm paying you to be an interpreter, that's all,' she had railed furiously at him. 'If I'd wanted your advice on anything else I'd have asked for it.'

She had fallen in love with the richly coloured glass stemware the moment she had seen it on the market stall, and she had been determined to order some for the shop, but Alex had done just about everything he could to dissuade her from doing so.

She knew why, of course. He had wanted her to give her order to his precious cousins. Talk about nepotism. Well, *she* had shown him that she had a mind of her own.

Beth could feel her face starting to grow hot with a

mixture of guilt and anger. She had been so determined to order the glassware that perhaps she had behaved in a way that was out of character for her. Perhaps? a cynical little inner voice demanded. There was no *perhaps* about it.

Hurriedly Beth concentrated on what the Customs and Excise official was telling her—namely that her long-awaited stemware had finally arrived and that they would be sending her the documentation which would enable her to collect it.

'You'll have to call for it in person since there are certain handling charges to be paid,' he told her.

'That's no problem,' Beth assured him happily, too thankful that her order had finally arrived to worry about the fact that she would probably have to spend half a day away from the shop in order to go through the formalities of collecting it.

'Good news?' Kelly asked her once she had finished her call.

'Very good news,' Beth confirmed. 'The stemware I ordered has finally arrived—thank goodness.'

'I'm looking forward to seeing it,' Kelly told her. 'We can use some of the glasses to celebrate Anna's new-found happiness. It *is* good to see her so happy,' Kelly added warmly.

'Mmm... It is. Dee and Ward are still circling one another a little bit warily, though, aren't they?'

'Just a little,' Kelly agreed. She had seen Dee the previous day and had raised with her the subject of Julian Cox.

'Doesn't Anna have any idea of where he is?' she had asked Dee.

'Apparently not,' Dee had confirmed. 'He's been

seen in Hong Kong, and then later in Singapore. He had investments in both places at one time, but it seems, in Singapore at least, that he was spending his time gambling.'

'Well, I'm just glad that he's gone out of our lives,' Kelly had told her truthfully.

Dee hadn't said anything.

'I'm going to need to drive over to Manchester Airport,' Beth told Kelly now, breaking into her thoughts. 'Can you hold the fort here for me when I do?'

'No problem,' Kelly assured her.

All in all their first year or so in business in Rye had been unexpectedly turbulent, but now, thank goodness, they had sailed into much smoother waters, both in their private lives and professionally.

'Mmm... I must say this order of yours is arriving just at the right time,' she praised Beth as she unwrapped her sandwich. 'We're getting pretty low on stock and I was beginning to think we might have to rush out and buy in.'

'Yes, we are getting pretty low,' Beth agreed. Her throat had gone uncomfortably tight. She still hadn't admitted to Kelly just how much of their partnership funds she had invested in her Czech purchases. On her return from Prague, rather than cast a shadow on Kelly's happiness with Brough, Beth had kept the exact details of what had happened and how much she had purchased to herself, but now, thankfully, she could stop worrying quite so much. At last, at last the order had arrived, and Beth knew that once it was displayed it would simply walk off their shelves.

Oh, yes, everything was quite definitely going to be

alright now, proving that she had been right to ignore all of Alex's dire warnings.

Yes, everything was going to work out fine now!

HARLEQUIN PRESENTS®

Seduction

SWEET REVENGE

They wanted to get even. Instead they got...married!

by bestselling author

Penny Jordan

Don't miss Penny Jordan's latest enthralling miniseries about four special women. Kelly, Anna, Beth and Dee share a bond of friendship and a burning desire to avenge a wrong. But in their quest for revenge, they each discover an even stronger emotion.
Love.

Look out for all four books in Harlequin Presents®:

November 1999
THE MISTRESS ASSIGNMENT

December 1999
LOVER BY DECEPTION

January 2000
A TREACHEROUS SEDUCTION

February 2000
THE MARRIAGE RESOLUTION

Available at your favorite retail outlet.

HARLEQUIN®
Makes any time special ™

London's streets aren't just paved with gold—they're home to three of the world's most eligible bachelors!

You can meet these gorgeous men, and the women who steal their hearts, in:

NOTTING HILL GROOMS

Look out for these tantalizing romances set in London's exclusive Notting Hill, written by highly acclaimed authors who, between them, have sold more than 35 million books worldwide!

Irresistible Temptation by Sara Craven
Harlequin Presents® #2077
On sale December 1999

Reform of the Playboy by Mary Lyons
Harlequin Presents® #2083
On sale January 2000

The Millionaire Affair by Sophie Weston
Harlequin Presents® #2089
On sale February 2000

Available wherever Harlequin books are sold.

HARLEQUIN®
Makes any time special ™